Pierre-Jean de Smet

New Indian Sketches

Pierre-Jean de Smet

New Indian Sketches

ISBN/EAN: 9783337010218

Printed in Europe, USA, Canada, Australia, Japan

Cover: Foto ©Andreas Hilbeck / pixelio.de

More available books at **www.hansebooks.com**

NEW INDIAN SKETCHES.

BY

REV. P. J. DE SMET, S.J.

* * *

NEW YORK:

D. & J. SADLIER & CO., 31 BARCLAY-ST.

BOSTON—128 FEDERAL-STREET.

MONTREAL—COR. NOTRE-DAME AND ST. FRANCIS XAVIER STS.

1863.

PREFACE.

THE holy life of Catharine Tehgahkwita, the saintly virgin of the Mohawk, is well known; and the odor of her virtues is still fresh on the banks of the St. Lawrence, where she edified all by her life, and aided so many after her death. Among the sketches of Father De Smet, published recently in Belgium, is a short memoir of Louise Sighouin, a holy woman of the tribe of the Cœur-d'Alênes, which shows us another example of high sanctity attained in an Indian wigwam, and affords us a model and a patron through whom we may piously expect that God will grant favors for the glory of his servant and the salvation of souls. The biography is one that cannot fail to touch and instruct all.

1*

To it we have added some of the more recent sketches of the pious missionary, whose letters are always so much esteemed, and a catechism of the Flathead Indians, to give some idea of the mode of instruction adopted by our missionaries, and the difficulty inherent in all the Indian languages of expressing religious thoughts. The illustrations in this work are from drawings by Father Point, whose pencil has preserved so many scenes and characters of the Rocky Mountains. They are the Baptism of Louise, and her venerated Grave.

S.

CONTENTS.

———◆———

LIFE OF LOUISE SIGHOUIN.

INDIAN SKETCHES

LOUISE SIGHOUIN,

AN INDIAN WOMAN OF THE CŒUR-D'ALÊNE
TRIBE,

WHO DIED IN THE ODOR OF SANCTITY IN 1853.

———•◦•◆•——— ··

CHAPTER I.

CHILDHOOD AND BAPTISM OF LOUISE.

LOUISE SIGHOUIN, of the tribe of Skizoumish or
Cœur-d'Alênes, daughter of the chief of the tribe,
was endowed with the noblest qualities of mind and
heart, which won her the esteem and respect not
only of all her nation, but also of the neighboring
tribes and of all whites who had an opportunity of
knowing her. A poor and humble child, but rich
in virtue and exalted in grace, Louise flowered in
the desert like a lily amid thorns. She was an oasis
amid a sterile waste; she was a light amid the
shades of death. Like the poor woman in the Gospel, she had sought and found the lost treasure, and

she carefully preserved it all the days of her life to her latest breath.

Before her baptism, even, she was remarkable for her rare modesty and reserve, great gentleness, and a solid judgment. Her words were everywhere listened to with admiration and pleasure, and her company sought in all families.

In October, 1841, a new era was preparing for her. In the course of the missions which I was then giving in the upper parts of the Rocky Mountains, I met for the first time three families of Cœur-d'Alênes, returning from the bison hunt on the plains of the upper Missouri. They joined my little band, and we travelled together. I found them mild, affable, polite in disposition, and above all very eager for the word of God. For several consecutive days I conversed with them on different points of faith and on the Church. After an instruction on the importance and necessity of baptism, they earnestly implored me to grant that favor to three of their little children. They were the first fruits of this tribe. When these families parted with us, all testified the most lively gratitude for what they had heard and learned with happiness: they assured me that the whole tribe would willingly accept the beautiful word of the Great Spirit, which I had announced to them, and they gave me a most pressing invitation to visit them at the earliest moment in order to instruct them.

Six months after, in April, 1842, I proceeded to their quarters. My good Cœur-d'Alênes, who had been my travelling companions, had admirably prepared the way for my visit, and infused into all their countrymen an eager desire to hear the good tidings of the Gospel. In consequence of the account which they gave, the chiefs had already hastened to depute to St. Mary's Mission several young men, selected from the most intelligent, in order to ask for missionaries to instruct them in the holy truths of religion.

The tidings of my coming soon spread through all the country. The Indians were to be seen flocking from all sides, through forest and plain, by the rivers and the great lake, to meet me, and hear the law of God from the very lips of a Black Gown. My visit, consequently, had the most beneficial results. I baptized all the little children in the tribe and a good number of adults, who had hastened with holy avidity to come and receive the mustard seed mentioned in the Gospel.

Among these was good Louise Sighouin. Enlightened by a special grace, and wishing to turn to the glory of God and the good of souls the rank which she occupied and the universal esteem she had acquired in the whole tribe, she used all her influence to induce a great number of families to follow her to the rendezvous, which was the great Lake Cœur-d'Alêne, in order to hear there the good and consoling word of the Gospel. From the very **first** she showed the greatest **avidity for it; at all times** was she most assiduous at the instructions of **the** missionary. Aided by his advice and counsels, **she** was seen advancing with a sure and rapid step, zealously and fervently in the path that was later to lead **her** to Christian perfection. Regenerated in the holy waters of baptism, where she **received the name** of Louise, she seemed to have **reached the** summit of her desires, and to think only of wearing unsullied **the** white **robe which** she had received, of keeping well trimmed on earth the flaming light that she had held in her hands, and of which from that moment she had seemed to realize and comprehend the sublime significance; in fine, of showing herself faithful and grateful to God for the great favors which he had deigned to grant to her.

CHAPTER II.

LOUISE'S ZEAL FOR THE CONVERSION OF HER TRIBE,
AND HER STRUGGLES WITH THE MEDICINE-MEN.

Soon after this she resolved to devote herself
entirely to the service of the missionaries who had
come to labor in the territory of the Cœur-d'Alênes.
With this view she generously renounced her native
spot, the guidance of her father, the society of her
relatives and acquaintances, to be with the missionaries at the first, and then at the second mission
station established in those countries. " I will follow
the Black Gowns," she often said, "to the end of
the world, for fear that death should surprise and
strike me far from them, and thus deprive me of the
help of the holy sacraments, and the salutary counsels of the Fathers. I wish to profit by their presence and their instructions to learn to know the
Great Spirit well, to serve him faithfully, and to
love him with all my heart."

This desire, or rather this ardent thirst to hear
the word of Eternal Life, never for a moment diminished in Louise. Sooner than be wanting to the
fidelity of her promises and her pious resolutions,
she subjected herself, with unlimited confidence in
God and with a holy ardor, to the severest trials

2

and greatest sacrifices. **From** the time **of** her conversion, **during** the whole residue **of her life,** she lived by **choice** and predilection in great poverty and in privations of every kind, never seeking to diminish them by the assistance of others, and without ever letting the slightest murmur escape her. **As St. Paul** lays it down, she seemed to profess " to know only Jesus Christ, and him crucified."

The zeal and fervor in the service **of God,** which she manifested immediately after her baptism, were the unfailing tokens of a predestined soul, filled with extraordinary gifts from heaven. **These privileged** favors were manifested in all their light by her admirable gentleness, which the greatest **opposition** could not disturb, by her patience **under** every trial, **by** her truly angelic modesty, **by her** fervent and sustained piety. She seemed, **as it** were, absorbed in prayer, and nothing apparently could then distract her thoughts. **Such** was her avidity, her holy ardor, to hear the Word of God, that every time a new religious truth broke in its effulgence on her mind, a visible joy overspread her countenance **and** her whole person : to her it was the precious discovery of a hidden treasure, a living fountain to quench her thirst of heavenly truths, a bread of life giving her new vigor. Each time she sought to share her happiness, this bread, this fountain, this treasure, with all who were like her hungering for the divine Word.

An ardent and an untiring zeal for the salvation
of souls seemed ever to occupy her thoughts. She
employed all her leisure moments in the conversion
and instruction of numerous pagans in her village.
Neither the opposition which she encountered, nor
the obstacles which she met, nor the insults which
she received, nor the dangers to which **she** exposed
herself, naught could divert her from the holy work
which she had resolved to accomplish. Thus each
day was marked by **some new** triumph, by some
new increase of **the** number of **the children** of God
or of the catechumens.

Louise boldly attacked face to face, **the** most
formidable and dangerous adversaries of religion:
the ministers of Satan himself, the sorcerers or jugglers, commonly called among the Indians *medicine-
men*, who by their impostures and diabolical arts,
always impose on the simple and ignorant. They
are the most deadly enemies whom the missionaries
encounter, and must ever **combat in the bosom of
the Indian tribes.** They never cease by tricks **and
calumnies and lies to** throw obstacles **in** the **way of**
the missionary and **fetter** the progress of religion.
The presence of the priest **is** the more odious to
them **as** they know that their private interest, their
wealth, is at stake, and that their illicit gains will
vanish and cease on the manifestation of religious
truths. *Inde iræ !* Hence, their hatred and resent-
ment; hence, too, the incessant war **they** wage on

the ministers of the true faith, and the persecutions they incessantly excite against them, whenever they can exercise sufficient influence over their adherents. And on what a people did they exercise their influence, before the arrival of our missionaries in their country!

Father Point, a missionary among the Cœur-d'Alènes from 1842 to 1846, wrote of them as follows, in a letter printed in 1848. These details prove the civilizing tendency and power of religion.

"Not a quarter of a century since, the Cœur-d'Alènes were so hard-hearted, that to paint them to the life, the common sense of their first visitors found no expression more just than the singular name which they still bear; minds so limited, that while rendering divine worship to all the animals that they knew, they had no idea of the true God, nor of their soul, nor consequently of a future life; in fine, a race of men so degraded, that of the natural law, there survived among them only two or three very obscure notions, which few, very few attempted to reduce to practice. Yet it must be said to the credit of the tribe, that there were always in their midst elect souls, who never bent the knee to Baal. I know some, who from the very day when the true God was preached to them, never had to reproach themselves with the shadow of an infidelity."

Among these the most remarkable was our heroine, Louise. Rising above all human respect, she
always followed the advice of the missionary. As
long as the wily medicine-men existed, she untiringly
opposed and exposed them. She boldly entered
their lodges, and with or without their leave, spoke
to them of the great truths of religion, alone true
and divine, exhorting them to follow it, in order to
avoid the terrible judgments of God, hell with its
frightful torments. She did this with such energetic fortitude, and such peremptory arguments,
that their obstinacy was shaken and their obduracy
softened.

Endowed with a heart and a courage above her
sex, Louise feared neither the sneers nor the threats
of these deceitful and embittered charlatans. Ac-
cordingly, the Almighty blessed the efforts of this
"valiant woman" of the wilderness, and always
crowned them with such extraordinary success, that
in a short time the medicine-men and their silly
juggleries fell into complete contempt. "In fine,"
wrote Father Point again, "from Christmas to Can-
dlemas, the missionary's fire was kept up with all
that remained of the ancient "medicine." It was a
beautiful sight to behold the principal supporters of
it, with their own hands destroy the wretched instruments which hell had employed, to deceive their
ignorance or give credit to their impostures. And
in the long winter evenings, how many birds'

feathers, wolves' tails, feet of hinds, hoofs of deers, bits
of cloth, wooden images, and other superstitious
objects were sacrificed!

Among Louise's chief conquests, they especially
mention the conversion of Nâtatken, one of the
principal leaders of the idolatrous sect.   He resisted
stubbornly; but at last, touched by the good example of all the converts, and above all, by the exemplary life of Louise's family, with which he was
connected by blood, he yielded to the earnest
exhortations, the sweet and persuasive words of the
young girl, and opening his heart to the grace of
our Lord after having been long a rebel, he came
like a timid lamb to the humble fold of the Good
Shepherd.   Louise devoted herself with the utmost
care to the instruction of the new catechumen, and
formed him to a kind of apostolic work in his tribe.
Till then a great master of Indian sorcery, he listened to and followed her wise counsels and instructions with the docility of a child; and after all the
necessary trials, Louise led him, humble and con-
trite, with his wife and children, to the feet of the
priest, to receive the sacrament of regeneration.
Nâtatken received the name of Isidore. He soon
became very zealous and very fervent. Endowed
with native eloquence, he unceasingly exhorted his
companions to convert and persevere in the faith,
and in the holy practices which religion imposes on
her children. He gave the example himself. He

remained faithful to the grace of the Lord till his
death, which was as edifying as consoling.

Emotestsulem, one of the great chiefs of the tribe,
after having been baptized under the name of Peter
Ignatius, had unfortunately relapsed into gambling,
the ordinary forerunner of apostasy among the
Indians. As soon as Louise heard this sad news,
although she was at a distance of two days' march,
she resolved to go to his town and find him so as
to endeavor to bring him back to his duties. She
set before his eyes the scandal which his conduct
occasioned in the tribe, the injustice of his course,
and the danger to which he exposed his faith. She
spoke to him with energy. Such was the authority
that Louise had acquired by her great charity and
exemplary life, such was the respect which she
commanded from all, that the great chief hearkened
to her with the submission of a child, and went to
cast himself at the feet of the priest in the tribunal
of penance, to repair the scandal and be reconciled
to God.

These two incidents, the conversion of Nâtatken
and that of Emotestsulem, will surprise all who
know how reluctant the Indians, and especially
their chiefs, are to receive correction, especially
when it is administered by a woman.

Let us say a few words of the famous sect of
jugglers or sorcerers, whom our modern spiritualists
have begun to style mediums. This sect is spread

over all the Indian tribes of both Americas, from the Esquimaux, who inhabit the Arctic regions, to the extremity of Patagonia.

All historians agree in saying, that the most perverse and wicked men in all the tribes are the medicine-men. Before their conversion to the faith, as well as everywhere else among the Indian tribes, each Cœur-d'Alêne had his *manitou* (tutelary spirit or divinity). To this manitou the Indian addresses his prayer or supplication, and offers his sacrifices, when he is in any danger, sets out for war, or goes fishing or hunting, as well as in every other enterprise in which he is about to engage, in order to obtain success or some extraordinary favor. He believes that he can ask every thing of his manitou, reasonable or unreasonable, good or bad. To obtain favors, he must be able to handle the bow and arrow, and although initiation to the manitou is considered as the most important act of life, the adept is required to submit to ceremonies and practices which are generally very difficult and often very painful. The young man after making profound incisions on the fleshy parts of the body, or after a rigorous fast, is supposed to discover in his dreams the form or resemblance under which the manitou manifests himself. During his whole life he is bound to bear the image or a mark of it; and on all occasions he must present his offerings and address his prayers to him. His talisman is the feather or beak of a bird, the claw or tooth of an animal, a root, a herb, a fruit, a scale, a stone, no matter what. He believes that this tutelary spirit will protect him against the evil genii, who to injure the children of earth excite the winds and waves, lightning, thunder, and storm. This spirit protects him against the attacks of his enemies, and wild beasts, and in all diseases that come upon him.

If I mention these dangerous and diabolical superstitions, so profoundly rooted in the mind of the Indian, it is to display more clearly the courage, firmness, patience, and perseverance which Louise must have had to oppose them successfully and even overcome them. Louise prepared herself for the struggle by long prayers and frequent fasts, and fortified herself by her humility, by her fidelity to the grace of our Lord, who made use of her as a chosen instrument to crush the monstrous serpent beneath her feet, and expel him from her tribe. Nevertheless, the devil never sleeps, he is always sowing tares in the good field, as Holy Scripture tells us, he "goeth about like a roaring lion, seeking whom he may devour." We must always fly to the "Watch and pray," for we perceive always that some trace of the old leaven remains.

CHAPTER III.

LOUISE'S ZEAL FOR THE **INSTRUCTION OF** HER TRIBE.

As I have already remarked, Louise manifested
an ardent desire and an active perseverence in instructing herself in all that pertained to the word
of God and the holy practices of religion. She
sought in the first place to enrich her fair soul with
heavenly truths, and then with admirable zeal and
charity she endeavored to relieve the missionary in
his laborious toils and the continual fatigue he
encountered, especially in instructing old people
and children. Entirely wrapped up in her noble
calling, she would go several times in the day to
the priest, to set forth her doubts and ask an explanation of them, and light on some points either in
the prayers or in the catechism, which she wished
to fathom more deeply.

This constant assiduity and application to the
study of heavenly things, soon rendered her capable
of being the head teacher of the catechism, and
enabled her to instruct the underteachers with
great fruit. At every explanation and development
which she received from the missionary, she would
say ingenuously, " I thank the Great Spirit for the

beautiful alms which he has deigned to bestow on me," and she felt herself bound to impart her knowledge to all the catechumens, to make them partakers in her happiness. She set the example to those good mothers, of whom Father Point speaks in his letter, who, not satisfied with giving their children the food which they refused themselves, spent long evenings in breaking, not only to parents and friends, but also to strangers, eager to hear them, the bread of the divine word, gathered by them during the day. The missionary, sometimes present at the pious meetings of these good women, admired the spirit of God which animated them, and applied to them the promise of the prophet, " The Lord shall give the Word to them that preach good tidings with great power."—Ps. lxvii. 12. The patience and constancy which Louise displayed in the office of catechist, deserve the highest eulogy ; the salvation of souls was a work of predilection to her; the hours of the day seemed too short to satisfy her zeal, and she often consumed a good part of the night instructing her neighbor.

Amid all her occupations and exertions for the good of others, Louise never neglected the care and ordering of her own house. Her prayers, her good works, her words, and her good example had drawn down the blessings of heaven on her poor and humble abode, and this model cabin, great by the virtues which it enshrined, shone with radiance amid

all the other Indian lodges. Louise **had compre-**
hended at once and fully the whole extent **of the**
duties of a good wife and mother, duties till then
almost unknown to the Indians, among **whom,**
from the moment of leaving childhood, each **one**
becomes absolute master of himself and his actions.
By her conduct beyond reproach, by her motherly
vigilance over the behavior of her children, by the
simple and persuasive gentleness with which she
treated them on all occasions, Louise had inspired
them with the most profound respect and entire
confidence, and had so closely bound to her their
tender hearts, that a desire manifested, or a single
word from the lips of their good mother, **was an**
absolute order, a law for them, which they **accom-**
plished in all its requirements with eagerness **and joy.**

Louise attended the divine offices with **the great-**
est exactness. Although in delicate **health and**
often sick, she never failed to be present **at** all the
religious ceremonies in use in the Church; she
attended Mass, morning and evening prayers, the
expositions and benedictions of the Blessed Sacrament, and all the other practices of devotion. Her
modesty, her recollectedness, and her fervent prayers,
always served as an edifying example to all present.
She seemed at the summit of her happiness and joy,
every time that she was permitted to approach **the**
holy table; her preparation and thanksgiving often
took whole days.

In catechising and in church Louise fulfilled all the duties of parents to their children. Sitting in their midst, she watched over their conduct and their innocent bearing. Rarely was she severe; when there was any thing to reprehend, the correction was always made with a mother's tenderness and goodness, which won her the hearts not only of the children but also of their parents. She merited and received from all the tribe the beautiful name of *good grandmother.* Her counsels and corrections were always and by all received with respect, submission, and gratitude; and the happy results were seen in a complete and blessed change of the whole tribe, thus augmenting joy and happiness in all hearts.

Louise, although the best instructed in the truths of religion, nevertheless came regularly to attend the catechetical instructions which the missionary was accustomed to give the children daily. She could be seen sitting or standing outside the half-opened door, regardless of the weather, heat or cold, rain or snow. She wished to gather all the important points of each instruction for her own spiritual good and that of others.

When there was question of admitting an old man, a boy or girl to partake of the Sacraments, she prepared and instructed them for several days in her lodge, impressing them with the high importance of the grace which they were going to receive, and

the happiness which they were **going to enjoy.**
She then aided them with the greatest care **to**
examine their conscience. And that nothing should
be lacking in the preparation, she took them one by
one to the tribunal of penance, telling them:
"Here —— kneel at the feet of the Father, who
has the power to reconcile you to the Great Spirit.
Say the Confiteor with a great sorrow for your
offences. Confess your sins with profound humility."
She would then withdraw to a short distance to
wait for them, and then lead them to the foot of the
altar to receive the spotless Lamb, and be nourished
with the bread of angels. Louise did not leave
them till they had finished their thanksgiving. **She**
wished **to** supply in some sort the lack of memory
or capacity, when the parties seemed to **need it.**
For fear of being guilty of any grave omission, **the**
chiefs themselves, and many **of the** most esteemed
men in the nation, went regularly **to have** her
assistance in preparing for a worthy reception of
the Blessed Sacrament.

Among other pious practices introduced by Louise
in the mission, we are indebted to her for the following. On solemn days, the night previous to the
general communion, hymns are sung alternately,
sometimes in one lodge and sometimes in another,
with charming harmony. These pious **canticles**
have reference to **the** approaching day, which they
are preparing to celebrate worthily. On the eve of

the communion, the Indians arrange their exterior, and for most this is no small affair. They wash, clean, and mend the clothes or rags which scarcely cover them; they go and bathe in a retired part of the river, even on Christmas Eve and when the water is freezing. Each one keeps in his leather bag, which serves as a wardrobe (for they have no chests or drawers), a piece of linen or white cotton, or a colored handkerchief; the women and girls wear them as a veil, the men as a cravat. Their toilet as you see is very simple and very poor; but each does his best, even outwardly, to come worthily and with respect to the table of the Lord.

CHAPTER IV.

LOUISE'S CHARITY FOR THE SICK.—HER POVERTY.

AMONG all the virtues which distinguished Louise, and which she cherished and practised with so much zeal and ardor, shone forth especially her Christian charity to the sick and dying. Father Gazzoli, who has for many years directed that mission, assured me that during Louise's life, he never went to the bedside of a sick or dying person, without there meeting the Indian "Good Samaritan." She devoted herself to the continual service of the sick, and tended them with as much care, patience, and interest, as she could have bestowed on her own children and parents. While relieving their bodies with admirable and truly maternal charity, she never failed to think of their soul, and devoted herself with still greater zeal and fervor to heal its wounds, especially when the state of the patient's conscience seemed most to require it. She suggested pious thoughts, and recited with them acts of faith, hope, charity, contrition, resignation, and submission to the holy will of our Lord; she constantly exhorted them to have patience in their painful trials, in imitation of our Lord, who died on the cross to save us; in one word she faithfully served her God in the person of her neighbor, conformable to these words of the Gospel: "Amen, I say to you, as long as you did it to one of these, my least brethren, you did it to me."—Matt. xxv. 40. With no other recompense than what she expected from her divine Master, she fulfilled all the duties of an excellent nurse. This service she performed with as much exactness and devotedness, as an exemplary Sister of Mercy or Daughter of St. Vincent de Paul could have shown. On many occasions when she wished to exercise her voluntary mission of charity, she had to consent to great sacrifices, and almost heroic efforts over herself, to overcome her natural repugnance. Father Gazzoli relates that one day, according to his custom in certain circumstances, he invited Louise to accompany him to a patient, to aid him in the care which a most loathsome sore required. Such was the sight of the corrupt mass, that for the first time the repugnance of the courageous woman overcame her; she durst not touch it or do the least to dress it. The missionary perceived it, and opened the abscess himself. Some moments after, Louise expressed the most lively regret at having yielded to her feelings, and told him with humility and respect: "I am greatly ashamed, Father; my weakness got the better of me. I admire your charity. I lacked courage to imitate it." She atoned for what she had reproached herself with as a fault, and immediately began to nurse the sick man, and dressed his sore with the greatest assiduity for about two months, till he recovered. It was the first time, added Father Gazzoli, that good Sighouin shrunk from a charitable desire which he expressed, and it was the last. In the sequel and down to her death, under every circumstance, she continued to fulfil, with promptness and fidelity, the requests made by her pious director, and made by him to offer her occasions of victory and merit before God. She had completely triumphed over herself, and in her humble constancy at the bedside of the sick, the most loathsome cases seemed to her the most agreeable and attractive.

Amid Louise's noble acts of charity and patience, may be cited the care she took for several years of a poor child on whom all human miseries of mind and body seemed to accumulate. An orphan, destitute of every thing, crippled, blind, and what is worse, stubborn and ungovernable, such was Louise's adoptive child. Such a child was doubtless a rich windfall to exercise a saint. One day she told the missionary that she could not manage Ignatius (that was the orphan's name), and that he would not mind her in the least. The Father who supplied his food and clothing, thought that by threatening to make him fast, he might be reduced to submission; but when it was tried, Ignatius rolled up his shirt-sleeve, and showing his arm, said: "Look there, I am fat. I can fast." He was then eleven or twelve years old. Such was the disposition of the child on whom Louise lavished the care of a tender mother for several years, till God recalled the poor boy from this world.

Louise had a niece named Agatha, the only daughter of one of her sisters. She was, and justly so, her child of predilection. Pious, and ever attentive to her aunt's good advice and wise lessons, Agatha verified her name by her exemplary conduct, and by her example amid her young companions. She was well instructed in her catechism, and was preparing for her first communion; she had already presented herself at the tribunal of penance to make a good confession, when an attack of apoplexy deprived her of speech. She survived only one day, suffering greatly, but with admirable patience. Her death was a severe and painful trial to the heart of Louise, who long after still kept her loss fresh in her mind, yet she submitted perfectly to the divine will, and convinced that her niece had gone to a better world, she overcame her grief, and shed not a tear; on the contrary, she never ceased thanking the Almighty for the favor he had bestowed upon Agatha, by snatching her away from the dangers of earth to set her in his heavenly mansion.

Louise lived in great poverty; yet the slightest murmur never escaped her to show her wants or her

suffering. When the missionary was able to give
her any charity, he had first to ask her whether she
was not in some need, either of food or clothing.
She regarded as nothing the privations and voluntary poverty which she imposed on herself through
love for her divine Lord, and for her neighbor.
Her lodge, formed of flag-mats, stood beside the
house of prayer, or church, and near the poor cabin
of the missionaries. There in happiness and con-
tentment Louise found all her treasure, all her joy,
and the complete fulfilment of her pious desire.
There she unceasingly contemplated the home of
eternal rest, which the Lord has prepared for his
elect in heaven, and to which he alludes in the
words : "My kingdom is not of this world."—John,
xviii. 36. Those which the Acts of the Apostles
add : " In very deed, I perceive that God is not a
respecter of persons. But in every nature, he that
feareth him, and worketh justice is acceptable to
him" (Acts, x. 34), seemed perfectly realized in
poor Louise. From her conversion she faithfully
followed the career which Providence had traced
for her. Poverty with zeal and charity were her
joy. Amid the poor of her tribe she may be said
to have been the poorest, and always blessed God
for her lot. Thus it is, that as we read in St.
Mark, the "last shall be first." Sighouin fully
comprehended this maxim, and she is at once a
striking and consoling example of it. How glorious

and beautiful is the society of fervent Christians, in all ranks and conditions of life! By its heavenly doctrines, benevolence admirably tempers authority; justice and charity reign in all hearts; the great humbles himself without derogating from his dignity, and the poor, the lowly, even the poor Indian woman, not only does not fall into contempt, but is elevated by the consideration of a common origin, the hope of a common end, and the distribution of the same means; in the sight of heaven all are equal, for all are children of one same Father, and called, though in different ways, to the possession of a common heritage.

Behold, then, the humble Louise, a poor Indian woman, an obedient, charitable, and submissive Christian. Zeal for souls, zeal for the house of God devours her. Endowed with heroic constancy and courage, she surmounts all obstacles that oppose her generous designs. Where does she find her courage, her strength, her consolation, her happiness, if not in the love of her God, in an entire confidence in him, and a holy indifference in regard to all else? All her actions seem to express constantly these words: "God alone for me! . . . God alone to-day and forever! . . . God alone for all eternity!" She devoted herself entirely to the cause of God; her labors, her troubles, her pain, will receive their reward. "She hath chosen the better part, which shall not be taken away from her."—Luke x. 42.

CHAPTER V.

THE SPECIAL DEVOTION **OF LOUISE TO** THE CROSS
OF OUR LORD, **TO THE BLESSED** SACRAMENT, AND
TO THE SOULS **IN** PURGATORY.

LOUISE always manifested a great devotion to the
Holy Cross. In the sowing season, in order to
draw down God's blessing on the crop, she each
year presented to her spiritual director the seed-
corn, to ask him to bless it. She then went through
the great harvest field and the fields of the Indians,
digging up a little piece of ground in the shape **of
a cross** to plant her **grain** in. During the **whole**
time that she maintained this practice, **it was every**
year observed, that the crop was very abundant **and**
very fine, even when the neighbors all **around** lost
their grain. She had learned that heaven and
earth had been disunited, and that the Cross had
reconciled them ; that no one can enter into heaven
except by the way of the Cross. She sowed **her**
grain in the form of a cross, having implicit confidence that our Lord, who died on the cross, would
fructify **it.** The Cross was her refuge on earth ; it
was her strength and consolation till death. **We**
may here repeat those beautiful words of the vener-
able Bishop Challoner : " Jesus is delivered into the

hands of his executioners; his suffering, his igno-
miny begins; he dies on an infamous gibbet; and
he is no sooner lifted up, than *he draws all things to
him*. The Cross dispels the darkness that covered
the face of the earth : it unveils the great mystery
of life and death, of God, of our duties and our eternal destiny; in a word, in all that till then had been
hidden from the wisest of pagan antiquity. The Cross
teaches us to suffer for the cause of justice, to bear
wrongs for the glory of God, to die for his love.
How admirably has the Gospel been styled by St.
Paul *the word of the Cross*."

Louise had a tender devotion to the most Blessed
Sacrament of the altar. That great mystery of the
love of God, who deigns to lower, and as it were,
annihilate himself, and " whose delight is to be with
the children of men" (Prov., viii. 31), seemed to
touch the good Indian woman most profoundly,
and to fill her heart with the liveliest gratitude.
Every morning she attended the holy sacrifice of
the Mass with the greatest recollectedness. For a
long time she went regularly to the missionary's
cabin to ask explanations and instructions on the
Holy Sacrament of the altar, without his supposing
it to result from any motive but a desire of instruction. It was not till after the death of Louise, that
he learned that when she had fully comprehended
the meaning and seen the explanation of the principal ceremonies and rubrics in the celebration of

the most holy mystery, she composed **short prayers,** full of unction, like those found in our best prayer-books. I must remark here that this **practice** was then as **yet** unknown **by the** catechumens **among** the Indians, for the missionaries, especially **in the** first years that followed the establishment of the mission, were unable to go beyond the most elementary instructions on **the** points **of doctrine** of the most absolute necessity. But the **zeal of Louise** was by no means limited to her own soul; **she had** at the same time in view the spiritual good **and** advancement of her neighbor by all these **holy** practices. Gifted with an excellent memory, **she** communicated with care and eagerness to others all the instructions that she had received **on the holy** sacrifice **of the** Mass. The beautiful and **admirable** little prayers of which **I have just** spoken **were in** harmony with the different **parts of the** Mass, perfectly conformable to the spirit of the Church, full of sense and piety; they seemed dictated under the inspiration of the divine Master. We may say with all assurance and truth, that this useful work of Louise was far beyond the ordinary capacity and reach of a poor Indian.

Among the holy practices in which **Louise** displayed most zeal, fervor, and charity, and **which** always seemed dearest to her, all remarked **her** great devotion for the souls in purgatory. **All her** prayers, all her actions, all the merits that she

might obtain from God by her pious and active life,
were directed to this noble intention. She succeeded, too, after persevering efforts, in making the
whole tribe relish and adopt her beautiful devotion.
Every day, even during the rigorous season of winter, she proceeded to the cemetery to spend some
time there in prayer. When the household occupations of her poor family prevented her visiting it
by day, she went there late in the evening, or even
during the night. This was frequently the case.
It seems that hell endeavored to raise obstacles to
prayers so agreeable to heaven, and, at the same
time, deprive the souls in purgatory of so many
suffrages, and good Sighouin of all the merits she
daily laid up for herself. The fact was this. Before
relating it, I must observe that, in the whole tribe,
Louise was regarded as a brave and nowise timid
woman, and that on many occasions she gave
unequivocal proofs of her natural courage. And
yet it several times happened that when at prayer
in the cemetery, she would be seized with affright,
at the sight of fantastic figures that she seemed to
behold before her. Once the spectres appeared in
so frightful a manner, that, trembling with fear, she
ran back to the camp with loud cries. The men
immediately all flew to arms, as though a powerful
enemy had assailed the village. All were convinced
that the alarm given by Louise must have a real
foundation. Father Gazzoli, who relates the facts,

4

had much trouble in restoring order and tranquillity
in the camp; he succeeded however, by promising
to act as sentinel all night over his dear **Indians.**
The next day he recommended Louise not to be
disturbed in her prayers by the influence of such
fears; and in case the phantoms returned again to
molest her, to come, even though it were midnight,
and tell him, but no one else, so **as to** create a
panic in the village. On this occasion **as** ever, she
showed her obedience and submission; and although
the frightful visions returned from time to time, her
victory over the demon was complete. From **that**
time for several years, and down to the period **of**
her last illness, she calmly continued her pious **visits**
to the cemetery, exempt from all trouble **and all**
fear. **One** day the missionary **in an instruction,**
advised his flock **to remember the souls in** purgatory, especially after communion. Louise received
the recommendation as an advice from heaven, and
the first time she approached the holy table, she was
seen, after receiving the Blessed Sacrament, proceed-
ing to the cemetery at the head of all the commu-
nicants, where they spent a considerable time in
prayer for the relief of the faithful departed. **Her**
example greatly increased this beautiful **practice of**
Christian life; the greatest part of the Indians **were**
soon seen following their pious guide **to the** place
of rest; at last all **went.** This holy custom is still
observed.

CHAPTER VI.

LOUISE'S PENITENTIAL SPIRIT; HER HORROR OF SIN,
AND ZEAL TO PRESERVE OTHERS FROM IT.

OUR poor Indians have a very limited intelligence; their progress in religious instruction is very slow, retarded especially by the difficulty which the missionaries encounter in the language of the Indians, which is very rich to express whatever is material; but excessively poor in all that relates to the explanation of spiritual things. Hence, it happens that many of these poor people have not yet that salutary horror and shame for sin, which are so powerful a means to restrain men's passions. Thus a woman who has been unfaithful or rebellious to her husband will receive pardon the moment she shows sorrow for it. A man who has grossly insulted another, or done him a grievous wrong, will go and smoke the calumet of peace with the injured person, or enter his lodge, or give him an equivalent for the wrong committed. These reparations are generally received, and considered sufficient, and the offender recovers the good graces of the injured party. "The wound is covered," as they express it; that is to say, "All is forgotten." When any one commits a fault, secret or notorious,

he goes of his own accord to present himself to the
chief and ask to be whipped. "The whip has covered his fault," no one can then speak of it. The
missionary has sometimes to instruct them in the
confessional on this point; for the penitent would
come, and not accuse himself of grievous faults
known to the whole tribe. In vain will the confessor say : "You have been guilty of such or such
a sin, you must accuse yourself of it before God."
The penitent will reply : "Pardon, Father, I went
to the chief, and the sin you mention was covered
by the whip; the whip has covered my fault." I
mention this usage of the Cœur-d'Alênes, because
our good Louise sometimes presented herself to the
chief to be publicly whipped. But here the case
was different; she seized the opportunity in a spirit
of profound humility, always regarding herself as a
poor and enormous sinner, and at the same time
from a desire to satisfy her devotion to imitate our
Lord, by submitting to the cruel flagellation. Louise's faults were only of the nature of those of
which the Book of Proverbs speaks, when he says
that the "just man shall fall seven times and shall
rise again."—Prov. xxiv. 16. Nevertheless, what
she called her faults, caused her such regret and
confusion, that the missionary often found her bathed
in tears. At the least fault, her contrition was so
lively, and, at the same time, her veneration for the
Lodge of the Lord (the church) so profound, and

her respect for the cabin of the priest **so** sincere, that she durst not enter either till she had approached the tribunal of penance. We admired in her, too, that faith and that love of God, which, in the real sins and faults of others, made her share in their sorrow and shame.

A certain **member** of the tribe, blinded by passion, in spite of all the obstacles in the way of his illicit desires, had resolved to unite himself with a near relative of Louise's, and who was at the same time nearly related to himself. Among the Indians there is no power to prevent evil in such a case but argument; when this fails there is no means to which they can have recourse. The wretched man, deaf to all the advice of the chief and of his own friends, obdurately closing his ears to the exhortations of the missionary, had united himself to the object of his desires. The traits which I have already given of the pure soul of Louise, will speak sufficiently the grief and bitterness which this depravity in a near kinswoman must have caused her. She had already employed all the means of persuasion in her power, to prevent the union of these two miserable people. They had turned a deaf ear to her wholesome advice and counsel, as to all that others had offered. **One day** the pastor showed himself more than ordinarily troubled and afflicted at the depravity and obstinacy of his two lost sheep, and at the great scandal they gave the whole tribe.

He said publicly and vehemently, "We must put a stop to this at once. Let each one then implore the divine assistance, and beg the Almighty, that with as little delay as possible, he will aid to remove this great scandal from among us." Louise was present and heard the missionary's words. She was ignorant of the guilty man's threats, for he had resolved to repel by brute force and by arms, whoever would dare to prevent his retaining the object of his guilty love. Invested with courage above her strength, like the strong woman in the Scriptures, and full of confidence in God, brave Sighouin immediately started from the village over woods and mountains, and marched for several days to the spot where the two culprits had hidden themselves to hide their crime and infamy. She entered the lodge to the great surprise of the guilty pair. One rushed at her, whip in hand, the other threatened to strike her; but Louise addressed them on the misfortune of their state, in words so resolute, so energetic, so overwhelming, that they stood silent and confounded before her, and without difficulty she rescued from his hands the woman whom sin alone had made his partner. She took her to her own house, and kept her there till a dispensation was obtained, on which they were lawfully married. The charity and zeal of Louise aided from on high, thus came forth triumphant from a struggle as heroic as it was delicate.

In another and nearly similar case, a wretched
man drew his dagger to strike Louise, while loading
her with insulting words and terrible threats; but
the Christian heroine, with a calm and serene
brow, portrayed to him the enormity of his conduct,
his ingratitude to God, the scandal given to his
neighbor. " I have come here," she said, "for the
honor of God, and the salvation of your soul; I fear
nothing." Here below, life is but a short passage.
" The world passeth away," says the beloved Apostle, " and the concupiscence thereof. But he that
doth the will of God abideth forever."—1 John, ii.
17. Louise fully comprehended these maxims, she
never shrunk from any danger when the glory of the
Almighty was concerned.

Louise paid special attention to the young girls
of her tribe. She took care of their religious instruction, and diligently watched over their behavior. In the absence of their parents she made
them all lodge in her cabin of mats, and took the
entire direction of them. To understand this, it
will be necessary to make a little digression. An
Indian lodge of mats is a pretty commodious, though
not very attractive abode. It assumes all dimen-
sions, according to the number of persons to be
accommodated: a few more poles and mats are
added, and the arrangements are completed. Thus
Louise was able to make room for a considerable
number of beds for the children, for each one has

her blanket or buffalo-robe. Their tables are the bare ground. Their dishes, plates, and spoons, are pieces of bark or wood; their fingers serve for forks and their teeth for knives. It takes an Indian, at most, half an hour to change a lodge into **a large** hostelry, and furnish it to correspond. Thus Louise was able **to** see herself at the head **of a** numerous household who were her delight. How beautiful it was to contemplate **the** good Indian grandmother, tenderly loved and respected, amid her cherished children!

CHAPTER VII.

SICKNESS AND DEATH OF LOUISE.

WE may apply to Louise the beautiful words of the Scriptures: "Being made perfect in a short space, he fulfilled a long time."—Wisdom, iv. 13. After her vocation to the faith, she did not indeed live long years on the earth, but her years were full of merits before God. "She walked in the ways of the Lord with a rapid step." In all that she did, she constantly kept her eyes fixed on her heavenly home, awaiting those eternal goods of which the great Apostle speaks; she made noble efforts, and employed all her moments to embellish and enrich her soul with all Christian virtues. By her regular attendance at the instructions, by her constant spirit of prayer, by the practice of every species of good work, she increased more and more in the grace and knowledge of our Lord and sweet Saviour, Jesus Christ.

Her last illness left her the use of all her faculties, which she preserved to her last breath. She thus prepared for death with all the tranquillity of the just. Her prayer was fervent and uninterrupted; her patience superior to every trial. Entirely taken

up with the salvation of her soul, she seemed utterly
unmindful of the sufferings of her body; she sought
no relief, and never betrayed the least sign of impatience; she often tenderly kissed the cross, which
she always carried around her neck. The desire of
the Apostle " to be dissolved and to be with Christ"
(Phil. i. 23), seemed to be during her illness her
only motto and her only preoccupation.

" Always at the bedside of her who had so greatly
aided me in my visits to the sick, and who had
always served as my interpreter, and given me her
aid with the ignorant,—the spiritual directress, the
guardian angel of her whole tribe,—I had the happiness to witness this touching scene," says Father
Gazzoli, the spiritual director of Louise. " Her virtues had shone like a brilliant torch amid the
Indians; she had never sullied the white robe of
innocence which she had received in baptism. I
witnessed the great power of the Cross, which
displayed in the desert virtues till then unknown;
whiclr produces wherever it is planted so many
holy martyrs, so many confessors, so many virgins
and illustrious penitents. Here, amid these isolated
mountains, appears a poor Indian woman, whose
unshaken faith and firm hope render her superior to
trials of every kind. I desired to relieve her in
some way; she in obedience gratefully received
what I offered, yet without seeking or asking the
slightest relief or the slightest mitigation of her

pains, which she accepted as so many special graces
of our Lord."

Louise received from the hands of the minister
of God all the consolations of the Church, the Holy
Viaticum especially, with truly angelic piety and
consolation. She thanked our Lord in all the
humility of her soul, for the great favors which he
deigned to grant her in that last hour of her earthly
anguish, committing to his holy Providence her
crippled husband and beloved children. She then
made an effort to rally her little remaining strength,
to thank her spiritual director for all the care which
he constantly lavished on her, and especially in his
instructions; she especially commended to his spiritual care the charge of all her family. The words
which Louise addressed to her husband and her
grieving children were consoling, full of trust in
God's divine and paternal goodness, full of resignation to His holy will, and of firm hope to be one
day all united again in their heavenly home. At
last she turned to those who surrounded her death-
bed, happy witnesses of all these edifying scenes,
which the just dying in the Lord present to the
living, and which realize the words of Holy Writ:
" Blessed are the dead who die in the Lord."—Apoc.
xiv. 13. She begged those around to intone in their
language the touching hymn in honor of the souls
in purgatory, and accompanied it herself in a
feeble and dying voice scarcely perceptible. They

were still singing it when Louise, unperceived by any, slept calmly in our Lord.

Her beautiful soul had taken its heavenward flight. She happily left the place of trouble, misery, and death, to pass to an abode of glory and peace, the delights whereof are eternal. In her were fulfilled what St. James teaches us when he says: "Blessed is the man that endureth temptation, for when he hath been proved, he shall receive the crown of life, which God hath promised to them that love him."—St. James, i. 12. In the pleasing hope that henceforth the eternal crown is her lot, with the deep-seated trust in her power with God, we addressed to her in heaven our poor prayers: "O Louise, intercede with God for him who conferred baptism on you, and was your spiritual director; for your husband, for your children, and and for all your dear Skizoumish. Obtain for us all the grace of perseverance in the holy service of our Lord. Amen."

I then addressed those around:

"Skizoumish! the example of the pious Sighouin is in your midst, we must profit by it. Henceforth she belongs to the whole nation, for she is the common beloved mother. As we all one day desire to share the glorious reward which she has just obtained by her virtues and good works, we must all follow the path which she has traced for us, and which leads to everlasting happiness. From the day of her baptism, in April, 1842, she constantly, night and day, devoted herself to your instruction. In the service of her God, she accepted with joy and eagerness, the privations, misery, contradictions, which it pleased Him to send her. In her this day are verified the words of the Lord addressed to the just: 'Because thou hast kept the word of my patience, I will also keep thee from the hour of temptation, which shall come upon the whole world to try them that dwell upon the earth.' "—Apoc. iii. 10.

The death of Louise Sighouin was the signal of a sudden desolation and a universal grief in the tribe, which lost a mother beloved by all, and especially by the children, a faithful friend to the whole nation, the comfort of the sick and afflicted, a guide and a support! The loss was immense, we avow. Yet this mourning was that of a Christian people, and not that of a perverse and unbelieving world, that has no hope beyond the grave. Amid this Indian tribe was renewed the salutary sadness that we ordinarily admire at the death of the just, whose memory is ever dear and in benediction, according to the words of the Holy Ghost: " O how beautiful is the chaste generation with glory: for the memory thereof is immortal: because it is known both with God and with men."—Wisdom, iv. 1.

The minister of the Lord was still reciting the

last prayers of the Church, invoking the angels and
saints to receive the soul of her who had just ex-
pired, to present it at the throne of the Most High,
when one of those kneeling beside him, ran out
crying : "Sighouin, good Sighouin is dead !"   The
cry was taken up and echoed in the valley and in
the foot of the high mountains which encircle the
Residence of the Sacred Heart.   The Indians ran
up in crowds around the lodge of the departed.   In
their impatience to gratify their desire of gazing
once more on the pious woman, the lodge was
invaded, but it was too small to hold them all, the
mats were torn from the poles; the lodge thus
opened on all sides, enabled the crowd of spectators
to satisfy their pious wish, and they gazed in ad-
miring silence on the last sleep of Louise.

It is a custom of the Indians for the relatives and
friends of a deceased person to assemble in his lodge
after his death.   When the missionary, after reciting the prayers of the Church, leaves the lodge,
he says : "Pray, my children, for the repose of his
soul," and adds some words suited to the circumstances.   Then, on a signal from one of the nearest
relatives of the deceased, all present burst into tears
and groans, either real or feigned, or rather they
begin lamentations, often forced, and extorted rather
by the usual ceremony, than by a real sorrow
caused by the loss of the deceased.   On Louise's
death the scene of mourning was far different: it

was doubtless sincere. Father Gazzoli thus relates
it: " I was an eyewitness, moved to tears by all that
passed. My emotion kept increasing, especially
when, even before the end of the prayers, universal
cries and tears, interrupted by sobs, announced
clearly that no ceremony was enacting here, but,
on the contrary, they had assembled to pay a just
tribute of gratitude and admiration to Louise's
virtues, and to relieve the lively grief caused by her
loss."

It must not be imagined that sunset, on this as
on other occasions, put an end to these demonstra-
tions of sorrow, regret, veneration, and love, displayed over the mortal remains of good Louise:
they rather increased. The Indians immediately
put up a vast lodge, which they illuminated by a fire
of resinous wood. The body, becomingly wrapped
in skins of wild animals, was respectfully laid upon
a bed of straw; a great number watch around, and
recite prayers aloud during the whole night. The
pious ceremonies of that night were till then unex-
ampled in the country of the Cœur-d'Alênes. There
was on this occasion a most touching, edifying, and
extraordinary unanimity. Men, women, and children, were seen surrounding with equal eagerness
the corpse of Louise, unable to tear themselves from
her whom they called by so many titles, their *mother*, their *guide*, and their *true friend*. Their prayers
and hymns were from time to time interrupted by

edifying discourses on the life and heroic virtues of the deceased; the principal chiefs of the **nation** were the first to retrace most touching pictures of them for the assembly.

The missionary, struck at **the** spectacle **of so** striking **a** testimony borne to virtue by a people possessed of such feeble ideas of it, believed it his duty to go and preside in this pious assembly. He proceeded to the lodge about midnight, **at** the moment **when the** eldest son of the deceased was making **a** panegyric on his beloved mother. **His** beautiful words, full of simple, unstudied, true eloquence, produced the liveliest sensation and emotion in all **his** auditory. The abundance of his **tears,** which **did** not cease to flow as long as he **spoke,** **prevented** him from continuing his long and interesting discourse. The missionary **then rose,** and while exhorting his good **Indians to imitate the** example of Louise, he expressed the sentiments of esteem and admiration which her virtues and good works had excited in his heart from his arrival in the Mission.

On the day succeeding the death of Louise, her body was carried in procession early in the morning to the church, accompanied by all the Indians of the camp. The labors of the harvest were not resumed all that day. All thought alone of **giving** in the most expressive manner a mark of their love, their esteem, and their grief, to the common mother of the tribe. **After a** solemn Mass of Requiem, and **all** the other funeral ceremonies of the Church, Father Gazzoli resolved **to** leave the body exposed during the **rest of the day, to** satisfy the pious zeal, **we might** almost **say** ever increasing devotion, of **the many** friends **of the** deceased. Her children, her family, all, in a word, constantly pressed around **the bier,** and seemed unable to tear themselves from it. It would **have** seemed too hard **and** too cruel to put an **end so soon to the** last expressions **of** affection of that religious assemblage, **of those** truly Christian hearts.

At **last the day** began **to** wane, and the shades **of** night **would soon** infold the valley. The missionary **had to make** an effort to overcome his own feelings, and to propose to his good children in Christ a separation so afflicting and so painful to their hearts. Yet it was the most favorable time to give the interment a funereal grandeur, and **a last tribute of** love and respect to the precious remains of Sighouin.

The funeral surpassed all expectation. The children alone, boys **and girls, as a proof of** their **innocent love, had thought of** preparing with care **a** large quantity of resinous splinters. These primitive torches in the hands of these children of nature, dressed chiefly in bear, wolf, jaguar, beaver, and otter skins, added to the ceremony, sad and mournful in itself, a peculiar air of wild majesty and savage grandeur, in keeping with the place and the

interesting occasion of the assemblage. Perfect
order was observed in the procession; modest piety
and holy silence reigned in the two long files, one
composed of men and the other of women, where
nothing was heard but the prayer and the chant.
The grave had been dug by the children and kin-
dred of Louise. Her simple and modest coffin was
the work of her youngest son. On reaching the
cemetery, the Indians ranged themselves in order
around the grave, and after the last funeral prayers
of the Church and some words of consolation from
the priest, the coffin was lowered. Each one present then threw a spadeful of earth into the grave,
pronouncing a prayer and a last adieu. This
touching ceremony, and the most trifling incidents .
of the great funeral, live in the memory of our
Cœur-d'Alênes. They repeat them and will repeat
them to their grandchildren; they will render ever
memorable this day of Christian sorrow, this religious
triumph conferred on a poor Indian woman of the
Skizoumish or Cœur-d'Alênes.

In the month of February, 1859, in one of my
visits to the husband of Louise, a poor old cripple,
unable for many years to walk without crutches, I
conversed with him on the holy life led by his wife
on earth, on her noble qualities, and the great
virtues of which she had given so striking an
example. I asked him what he had most loved
and admired in her. "Truly, Father," he replied,

"I cannot tell you in what Louise most excelled. From the blessed day on which you conferred baptism upon us, all was good and admirable in her life. Never to my knowledge was there the slightest shadow of a difference between us; not a syllable, not a word louder than another. When I was sick she carried me in the .canoe; if I could not use my hands, she cut my food and put it in my mouth. Louise served me like a guardian angel. Now I am an object of pity and compassion, for I am weak in mind. I loved to hear her consoling words, to listen to her wise counsels, to follow her salutary advice, for she was full of the wisdom and spirit of God. The Fathers taught her many beautiful prayers, and we recited them together with our children. Now I have no one to repeat those beautiful prayers to me, and I am to be pitied. Yet I never cease thanking the Lord for the favors which he has not ceased to bestow upon me. I submit myself to his holy will; my heart is always satisfied and calm."

The good old man has always been a subject of edification amid his tribe, universally loved and respected by all the nation. He is a man of the greatest simplicity and of very solid and fervent piety; nothing gives him greater pleasure than a conversation on holy things and on the great affair of salvation. You can never visit him without seeing the smile on his lips and without finding him at prayer, with his beads in his hands. He begins to say the rosary early in the morning; the first is offered to Mary to keep him in the holy grace of the Lord during the day; he recites the others either for the missionaries, for his family, for his tribe, or for some other intention. From the day of his baptism, he made it a duty to pray for me every day, and I feel the utmost gratitude to him.

Good Adolph, such is the name of Louise's husband, related to me among other things, that during his wife's life, when the village set out for the chase, or to get wild roots, and Louise went along with them, he felt very lonesome. When he saw Louise about to die, he told her: "If you die, it will be impossible for me to stay here; I shall find the time so long, I will go back to my own land." "Take care not to do so," returned Louise; "be very careful not to do so, Adolph! Do not remove from the house of the Lord (the church). As I die here, I wish you to remain here till you die. You will not be lonesome." Adolph remains faithful to to his wife's recommendation. His cabin is beside the church, and although alone the greater part of the time since the death of Louise, he has not felt the time tedious for a single moment. His beads and prayer are his greatest consolation, and his only delight.

On my recent visit to the Cœur-d'Alênes, I again

questioned the Indians, in order to obtain new
details as to the life of Louise Sighouin. The
answer was this : " After so many years it is difficult
to add any thing to these extraordinary facts, so
well known by all, except that from the time of her
baptism, her life was an act of continual charity."
And I can say, and all that read this narrative will
agree with me, that there is no exaggeration in this
summary remark. · It was a devotedness of every
day and every hour, a chain of links of little details
of mercy, which offer nothing very striking, unless it
be that untiring constancy, which for more than ten
years, was always prompt night and day in exer-
cising all works of charity, corporal and spiritual.
No one will better appreciate this martyrdom of
detail than those who are themselves devoted to it;
and if we consider that Louise was poor, infirm,
that she could only half understand the missionaries,
who as yet only stammered the language of the
Indians, no one will call in doubt the many graces
which Louise received, and the immense profit she
derived from the lessons of her Divine Master.
God had raised up Louise to be the assistant of the
apostolic men in the outset of their labors, when
they did not understand the language. It had
been the same at the mission of St. Ignatius. The
Almighty had given the missionaries the chief
Loyola to do among the Kalispels what Louise has
done among the Cœur-d'Alênes. Both were poor

and infirm; it was a lively faith which **animated**
their zeal; both devoted themselves to **their last**
sigh, and both were bitterly deplored **after their**
death.   Loyola displayed invincible firmness.   **"As**
long as I have a breath of life, my people must
walk uprightly," said **he; and** his **virtue alone** gave
him the authority to speak so.   Louise on the contrary had no support **in her zeal except her** admirable meekness, her unwearied **patience.**   Both
died about the same time, when the missionaries
began to be generally understood by the Indians.

I have all these circumstances from the missionaries on the spot, especially from the reverend and
worthy Father Gazzoli, nephew of the cardinal of
that name who died **in** 1858.   This Father **is at**
this moment Superior of the Mission of the Sacred
Heart among **the** Skizoumish **or Cœur-d'Alênes.**

In one of **my** letters written ten **years ago,** June
4, 1849, I said : " This extraordinary attention of
the Indians, and this avidity on their part for the
word of God, must seem surprising in a people who
appear to combine all moral and intellectual miseries.
But the spirit of the Lord breathes where it pleases
him, his graces and his light prompt and aid **men**
whom ignorance, rather than a perverse or disorderly
will, has rendered **evil.**   And that **same spirit**
which obliged **the** most rebellious to cry out **with**
St. Paul : ' Lord ! what wilt thou have me to do ?'
can often soften the fiercest hearts, inflame the

coldest, produce peace, justice, and joy, where
iniquity, trouble, and disorder reigned. The great
respect and attention which the poor Indians show
on all occasions to the missionary who comes to
announce to them the word of God, are a source of
great consolation and encouragement. He finds the
finger of God in the spontaneous manifestations of
these unhappy men." Since the Gospel has been
announced to the tribes of the Rocky Mountains,
the Lord has always had his chosen souls among
them. In the different missions, many neophytes
are distinguished by a zeal and piety truly worthy
of the primitive Christians, by a rare assiduity at
all religious exercises, by the faithful accomplish-
ment of all the duties of a good Christian, in a
word, by all the virtues which we have just seen in
their highest form in Louise Sighouin.

INDIAN SKETCHES.

SACRED HEART MISSION, 21st June, 1859.

I HAVE just received your kind letter of March 12th, 1858; it was more than a year on the way. I hasten to comply with your request by saying a word as to our labors. The language is the greatest difficulty. One must learn it as best he can. There is no written language, there are no interpreters, there is very little analogy with other tongues. The pronunciation is very harsh, the turn of thought is entirely different from ours. They have no abstract ideas, every thing is concrete. And with these elements it is necessary to create a religious, and even spiritual, phraseology: for the savages know nothing that is not material.

I have been here nearly fifteen years. I am not yet master of the language, and am far from flattering myself with the hope of becoming so. My catechist remarked to me the other day, "You pronounce like a child learning to talk : when you

6

speak of religion, we understand you well; but when you change the subject, it is another thing." That is all I want. I have at last succeeded in translating the catechism. I think it is nearly correct. You can hardly imagine what it cost me to do it. I have been constantly at work at it since my arrival here. I finished it only last winter. Nevertheless, it is very short; it has but fourteen lessons. It is based upon the first part of the Catechism of Lyons, which was in use in the diocese of St. Louis (of which this mission formed a part) upon our arrival. This catechism is printed, not on paper, but on the memory of the children : they know it all by heart, questions and answers, and they say two lessons of it every day after morning prayer; so that they say the whole of it once a week. The good will of these poor Indians is admirable; I never saw or heard of any thing to equal it. I am never tired of hearing them their catechism; on the contrary, it is my greatest pleasure. Oh, if you could have seen what passed here last winter, how your Reverence would love these poor savages, and how you would pray the Queen of Apostles to send them missionaries. Thirty children made their first communion together, and I cannot even yet think of the manner in which they prepared for it, without emotion.

From the end of November to Palm Sunday, on which day this ceremony took place, they had catechism at the church three times a day, and it was rare that one missed the exercise: besides this there was a repetition, every day, either before the chief or the catechist. Every time that I gave them permission to assemble in my apartment for more ample explanations, they crowded there, remaining in postures of the greatest discomfort for three-quarters of an hour or an hour at a time, without ceasing to give me the utmost attention. They never became weary. There was no end to private recitations among themselves, and little bands would everywhere be found retired and reciting the catechism. When visiting the sick in the evening, I was almost certain to hear, in some tent or other, groups of children reciting catechism, the more advanced helping the others; and this zeal for instruction increased rather than diminished.

During the month of January, the period of the great deer hunt, the children came to ask my permission to return to their parents: this period is that of harvest with them. How could I refuse them. They were actually suffering with hunger at the Mission; besides, their parents themselves had expressed the desire to see them. "How much holiday do you want?" "Four weeks." "I allow it." It was not too much. I see nothing very surprising in the fact that a boy, after a vacation of two months, may be glad to return to school. Soli-

tude and inaction have become wearisome to him.
But the case with my dusky children of the forest
is very different. At camp there is no want of
occupation or of companions, they have food in
abundance, which is rarely the case at the Mission.
This year, in particular, the scarcity has been great.
Nevertheless, they obtained of their parents the
permission to shorten their vacation by one half.
With their snow-shoes on their feet, and their
bundles on their backs, they made a distance of ten
leagues (28 miles English), crossing a mountain
covered with a thick forest, over soft snow. You
must be on the spot to know what are the fatigues
of such a journey. Judge of my surprise when I
saw them all enter my room at nightfall, worn out
with fatigue, but gay and happy. What motive
could induce them to leave the abundance they
were enjoying with their parents, to come to the
privations of the Mission? I know of no other
than their desire to be instructed in order to make
their first Communion. They knew well enough
that I had nothing to give them but the bread of
the Divine Word. For, be it said, by the way,
although I give catechism three hundred times a
year, I doubt whether there is a catechist in the
world more utterly deprived of the means of en-
couraging his pupils. Some prayer-beads would
have been a great reward, but I could give them
nothing but a medal to each as a memorial of their

first communion. I was almost tempted to regret my poverty. In Europe there are many pious souls to encourage poor children in like circumstances, but here, on the borders of the world, want has no witness but the missionary, who can give it only his sighs. The mines have ruined us, and it is precisely when prices have doubled, that our resources have diminished, so that instead of giving catechism, one is often obliged to rack one's brains to make both ends meet. All that I have said of my dear children is the exact truth, without exaggeration. I am no poet. However, I begin to fear that I shall be reminded of the fable of the owl and the eagle; so, though I have much yet to tell, I will stop here.

However I cannot but beg you, and those to whom you may communicate these lines, to recommend these dear children to our Lady of Fourvières, that she may obtain for them the gift of perseverance. They are exposed to many dangers. Not to speak of others, strong liquors have already found their way into the neighboring tribes: and I know that the wretches who make it their business thus to ruin the poor savages, boast that our people will not be able to resist the temptation more than the others. If their infernal predictions should be realized, you may see me again one day in Europe.

I do not know to whom to address myself to convey our thanks to the Ladies of the Sacred

Heart. We received, some years since, two sets of
very fine vestments, for our Church of the Sacred
Heart, from some unknown benefactors. I have
just learned that the present was from those ladies,
but I know not of what House. By the way, no
one sees our church without testifying his astonish-
ment. It is entirely the work of the Indians, except
the altars. It is a magnificent monument to the
faith of the Cœur-d'Alênes, who have given the lie
to their name by its erection. If it were finished,
it would be a handsome church even in Europe.
The design is by Father Ravalli. It is 90 feet long
by 40 wide. It has 28 pillars, $2\frac{1}{2}$ feet square by
25 feet in height. All the rest is of timber, and
in proportion. It was all cut, raised, and roofed by
the savages, under the direction of a Father; they
also filled it in, and built the foundation-walls,
which are from two to five feet high, and of proportionate thickness. The Indians brought the stones
from a distance of eight hundred feet, did all the
mason work, and would accept no recompense. It
is a great grief to us that we cannot finish it.
There are two fine altars, with handsome pictures
of the Sacred Heart and of the Blessed Virgin, but
all the rest is naked, without doors, windows, or
flooring, and not being framed in on the outside, I
fear it will rot before it is completed. The neophytes
have done their best: but in the absence of resources,
we cannot continue the work.

LETTER OF FATHER DE SMET.

St. Louis, Nov. 1, 1859.

REVEREND AND DEAR FATHER:

In accordance with your request, I proceed with great pleasure to give you some details of my **recent** journey.

On the 20th of May, 1858, **I** set out from **St.** Louis for the western portion of North America, **and** after an **absence** of about sixteen months, I returned to the point from whence I set out. During this interval, I had accompanied, as chaplain, an army sent out by the United States against the Mormons and the savages. I propose to give you some details of this double expedition. Not to fatigue you, I will endeavor to be brief. At best, **however,** my narrative will fill some pages, as my **recent** voyage **has been** very long. It exceeded fifteen thousand English miles, or five thousand leagues. I propose then **to** give you some details in regard to the different countries I have traversed, and the seas I have crossed, and of my visit to the savage tribes, my dear spiritual children of the Rocky Mountains, the Cœur-d'Alênes, Kalispels, Pends-d'Oreilles, Flatheads, and Koetenays; of my stay among the different tribes of the Great Plains of the Upper Missouri, and of the manner in which my time was spent in the army of the United States in quality of chaplain, and envoy extraordinary of that Government. These details, I venture to hope, will not be without interest for you, and they will form the subject of my little sketch.

Several years have passed, since the Mormons, that terrible sect of modern fanatics, flying from civilization, settled in the midst of an uninhabited wilderness. With hearts full of hate and bitterness, they never ceased on every occasion which presented itself, to agitate the country, provoke the inhabitants, and commit acts of robbery and murder against many travellers and adventurers from the United States. In September, 1857, one hundred and twenty emigrants from Arkansas, men, women, and children, are said to have been horribly massacred by the Mormons, in a place called the Mountain Meadows. These fanatics never ceased to defy the government, and announced that the day had arrived to avenge the death of their prophet, Joseph and his brother, and to retaliate the wrongs and acts of injustice and cruelty of which they pretended to have been the victims in the States of Missouri and Illinois, whence they had been forcibly expelled by the inhabitants.

On two different occasions, the governor and subaltern officers, sent by the President of the

United States, had met with such strong opposition from the Mormons in the attempt to accomplish their respective duties, that they were forced to quit the Territory of Utah, and to return to lay their complaints before the President. Congress resolved to send a third governor, accompanied, this time, by two thousand soldiers, who were to be followed by from two to four thousand others in the following spring of 1858. I accompanied the last-named expedition. On the 15th of May, 1858, the Minister of War wrote to me as follows:—

"The President is desirous to engage you to attend the army for Utah, to officiate as chaplain. In his opinion your services would be important in many respects to the public interest, particularly in the present condition of our affairs in Utah. Having sought information as to the proper person to be thus employed his attention has been directed to you, and he has instructed me to address you on the subject, in the hope that you may consider it not incompatible with your clerical duties or your personal feelings to yield to his request," &c.

The Reverend Father Provincial and all the other consultors, considering the circumstances, expressed themselves in favor of my accepting. I immediately set out for Fort Leavenworth, Kansas Territory, to join the army at that point. On the very day of my arrival, I took my place in the Seventh Regiment, composed of eight hundred men under the command of the excellent Colonel Morrison, whose staff was composed of a numerous **body** of superior officers of the line and engineers. General Harney, the commander-in-chief, and one of the most distinguished and most valiant generals of the United States, with great courtesy, installed me himself **in** my post. The brave colonel, though a Protestant, thanked him very heartily. " General," said he, "I thought myself highly honored when intrusted with the command of the engineers: to have attached to my command a representative of the ancient and venerable Church, I hold as **an** additional favor." General Harney then shook hands with me, with great kindness, bade me welcome to the army, and assured me that I should be left perfectly free in the exercise of my holy ministry among the soldiers. He kept his **word most** loyally, and in this he was seconded by all the officers. During the whole time that I was among them, I never met with the slightest obstacle in the discharge of my duties. The soldiers had always free access to my tent for confession and instruction. I had frequently the consolation of celebrating the holy sacrifice of the Mass early in the morning, and on each occasion, a large number of soldiers devoutly approached the holy table.

A word or two in regard to the character of the countries through which we passed, will perhaps be agreeable to you. I left Fort Leavenworth on the

1st of June, 1858, in the Seventh Regiment, commanded by the worthy Colonel Morrison. I had an opportunity of observing with admiration the extraordinary rapidity of the progress of civilization in Kansas. A space of 276 miles was already in great part occupied by white settlers. No further back than 1851, at the time of my return from the great council, held on the borders of the Platte or Nebraska river, the plains of Kansas were almost entirely without inhabitants, containing only a few scattered villages of Indians, living for the most part by the chase, by fishing, and on wild fruits and roots. But eight years have made an entire change: many towns and villages have sprung up, as it were, by enchantment; forges and mills of every kind are already very numerous; extensive and beautiful farms have been established in all directions with extraordinary rapidity and industry. The face of the country is entirely changed. In 1851, the antelope, the wild deer, and the wild goat, bounded at liberty over these extensive plains, nor is it much longer ago that these fields were the pasture of enormous herds of buffaloes; to-day they are in the possession of numerous droves of horned cattle, sheep and hogs, horses and mules. The fertile soil rewards a hundredfold the labors of the husbandman. Wheat, corn, barley, oats, flax, hemp, all sorts of garden stuff and all the fruits of the temperate zone, are produced there in

abundance. Emigration tends thither, and com-
merce follows in its tracks and acquires new importance every day.

Leavenworth is the principal town of Kansas
Territory. It contains already about ten thousand
souls, though it has sprung into existence within
the last six years. It is beautifully and advantage-
ously situated on the Missouri river. It has a
bishop, two Catholic churches, a convent with a
boarding-school and a day-school. There are already fifteen churches, twenty-three stations, sixteen
priests, five religious communities, and four manual-
labor schools for the Osage and Potawatomie Indians, which are under the care of our Fathers and
Religious Ladies of different orders.

The greater portion of the Territory is not thickly
wooded : the surface of the country, as a general
thing, is rolling and well adapted to agriculture ; it
is not unlike the billows of a vast ocean, suddenly
arrested in its flow and converted into solid land.
The air is fresh and wholesome. As one rises with
the elevations of the soil, the graceful undulation of
the alternating vale and hill contrast admirably with
the waving lines of walnut trees, oaks, and poplars,
which mark the course of each little river. The
banks of each stream are generally more or less
thickly wooded. We ascended the valley of the
Little Blue for three days, making a distance of
fifty-three miles. The names of the principal plants

which attract the attention of the botanist in the plains of Kansas, are : the *anothera*, with its brilliant yellow flowers, the *amorpha* and *artemisia*, the *commelina*, the blue and purple *lupin*, different forms and species of *cactus*, the *pradescantia*, the *mimosa*, and the white *mimulus*. The waters of the Little Blue are left at a distance of 275 miles from Fort Leavenworth. Continuing the route from that point, you cross elevated prairies of a distance of twenty-six miles, and enter the great valley of the Nebraska or Platte river, at the distance of fifteen miles from Fort Kearney. This river, up to its two forks, is about three thousand yards wide ; its waters are yellowish and muddy in the spring freshets, and resemble those of the Missouri and the Mississippi ; it is not so deep as those streams ; its current is very rapid. Fort Kearney is rather insignificant. It consists of three or four frame houses and several made of *adobes*, a kind of coarse brick baked in the sun. The Government has a military post there for the tranquillity of the country, and to provide for the safety of travellers crossing the desert to go to California, Oregon, and the Territories of Utah and Washington.

A great number of Pawnee Indians were encamped at a little distance from the Fort. I came near witnessing a battle between them and a war party of Arapahoes, who, favored by the night, had succeeded in approaching the camp unseen almost forty strong. The Pawnees had just let their horses loose at break of day, when the enemy, with loud cries, rushed into the drove, and carried away many hundreds with them **at** full gallop. The **alarm** immediately spread throughout the camp. The Pawnees, indifferently armed and almost naked, rushed to the pursuit of the Arapahoes, caught up with them, and **a** combat more noisy than bloody took place. A **young** Pawnee chief, **the** most impetuous of his band, was killed and three of his companions wounded. The Arapahoes lost one killed and many wounded. Desirous to stop the combat, I hurried to the scene of battle with an aid-de-camp **of** the general, but all was over **when** we arrived; the Pawnees were returning **with their** dead and wounded and all **the stolen horses. On** their return **to** camp, nothing was **heard but cries of** sorrow, rage, and despair, **with threats** and vociferations against their enemies. It was a harrowing scene. The deceased warrior was decorated and painted with **all the** marks of distinction of a great brave, and loaded with his finest ornaments. They placed him in the grave amid the acclamations **and** lamentations of the whole tribe.

The next day the Pawnee-Loups invited **me to their camp.** I found there two French **Creoles,** old acquaintances of **mine, of the Rocky Mountains.** They received me with the greatest kindness, and desired to act as my interpreters. I had a long conference on religion with these poor, unhappy savages. They listened with the most earnest attention. After the instruction they presented to me 208 little children, and very earnestly begged me to regenerate them in the holy waters of baptism. These savages have been the terror of travellers obliged to pass through their territory; for many years their character has been that of thieves, drunkards, and ruffians, and they are brutalized by drink, which they readily obtain, owing to their proximity to the frontiers of civilization. This accursed traffic has always and everywhere been the ruin of the Indian tribes, and it leads to their rapid extinction.

Two days' march above Fort Kearney, at a place called Cottonwood Springs, I found thirty lodges of Ogallallas, a Sioux or Dacotah tribe. At their request I baptized all their children. In 1851, at the Great Council on the Platte, I had brought them the same blessing. They told me that a great number of their children had died since, carried off by epidemics, which had raged among the nomadic tribes of the plains. They are much consoled at the thought of the happiness which children obtain by holy baptism. They know its high importance, and appreciate it as the greatest favor which they can receive.

General Harney had many friendly conferences with the Pawnees, the Ogallallas, and the Sheyennes, in which he strongly advised them to cease molesting the whites who might pass through their borders, adding that on this condition alone could they remain at peace with the United States.

I have so often spoken of the buffalo in my letters, that this time I might pass him by in silence. However, I will mention it for the purpose of saying that the race is not extinct in these parts, though it is becoming more rare to find buffaloes on the highway across the plains, which its instinct must have taught it to avoid. We met our first herds of this noble animal in the neighborhood of Fort Kearney. The sight created great excitement among those soldiers who had not visited the plains before, and they burned to bring down one or two. Armed, as they were, with the famous Minié rifles, they might have made a good hunt, had they not been on foot, while the buffaloes were at full gallop; it was, therefore, impossible to get near them. They fired, however, at a distance of two hundred or three hundred yards. A single buffalo was wounded in the leg. Its wound compelled it to lag behind, and he became the target of all our men. A confused sound of cries and rifle shots arose, as if the last hour had come for the last buffalo. Riddled with balls, his tongue lolling out, the blood streaming from his throat and nostrils, the poor brute fell at last. To cut him up and distribute the meat was the work of a moment. Never was buffalo more rapidly transformed into steak and soup,—every one would have his piece.

While these things were going on, Captain P——, mounted on a fine horse, approached a bull, already terrified by the rifle shots and the terrible noise of our soldiers, who were novices to the chase, and fired at him twice almost point blank. The buffalo and the horse stopped at the same instant. In spite of all his efforts, Captain P—— could not make his horse, unaccustomed to the hunt, advance a single step, and the furious buffalo plunged both horns into his flank and threw him down dead. In this critical moment the courageous rider did not lose his presence of mind : he leaped from his horse over the buffalo's back, gave him two more bullets from his six-shooter, and completely baffled him. The captain then fled to a gully, which was luckily both deep and near at hand. The buffalo, unable to follow him, abandoned his persecutor, who returned to camp with his horse's saddle on his back. A horse must be well trained to hunt the buffalo, and must be trained specially for buffalo hunting : otherwise the danger is very great, and the consequence may be fatal.

During the months of June and July, tempests and falls of rain and hail are very frequent, and almost of daily occurrence, towards evening in the valley of the Platte, which is the country of storms and whirlwinds *par excellence*. The gathering of

these storms can be noticed at a great distance, as at
sea.   At first, light spots of clouds are observed on
the horizon, which are followed by dark masses
of cloud, which move along in succession, crowding
one upon another, and spreading over the sky with
extraordinary rapidity, they approach and cross
each other; they burst and **pour forth** torrents of
water, which drench the valleys, **or volleys** of hail
which crush the herbs and flowers; **the storm-**
clouds then disappear as rapidly **as** they have come.
"Every evil has its remedy," says the old proverb,
and these hurricanes, storms, and heavy rains, serve
the purpose of cooling and purifying the atmosphere, which at this season would become insup-
portable but **for** this circumstance.   The mercury
often rises to one hundred degrees of Fahrenheit in
the shade.   The water does **not rest long** on the
surface of the **soil:** it is absorbed **almost as it** falls,
on account of the very porous character of **the**
earth of the valley and its sandy bottom.   Travellers, in camps a little removed from the river,
always dig wells; the water is everywhere found at
a depth of two or three feet.   This water, though
cold and clear, **must** be unwholesome, and frequently
causes severe sickness.   Graves abound in **these**
regions, and the mortal remains of a vast **number**
of emigrants repose there.   With these emigrants
have also sunk beneath the **valley of the** Platte
that ardent thirst **for gold, those** desires and am-

bitious projects for wealth, greatness, and pleasure, which devoured them, and drove them towards the distant regions of California, Pike's Peak, and Frazer. Death met them far from their Penates, and they are buried in these desert strands. How uncertain are the affairs of this world! Man makes his plans; he builds his castles in the air; he counts upon a future which does not belong to him: he proposes, but God disposes, and cuts the thread of life in the midst of these vain hopes.

The most remarkable thing that I met on **this** occasion on the highway of the prairies, ordinarily **so** lonely, were the long wagon trains engaged in transporting to Utah provisions and stores of **war.** **If** the journals of the day may be believed, these cost the Government fifteen millions. Each train consisted of twenty-six wagons, each wagon drawn by six yoke of oxen, and containing near five thousand pounds. The Quarter-master-general made the calculation, and told me that the whole train **would** make a line of about fifty miles. We passed **every day** some wagons of this immense train. **Each** wagon marked with a name as in the case of ships, and these names served to furnish amusement to the passer-by; the caprices of the captains in this respect having imposed upon the wagons such names as the *Constitution*, the *President*, the *Great Republic*, the *King of Bavaria, Lola Montes, Louis Napoleon, Dan. O'Connell, Old Kentuck*, &c., &c.

These were daubed in great letters on each side of
the carriage.   On the plains, the wagoner assumes
the style of *captain*, being placed in command of
his wagon **and** twelve oxen.   The **master-wagoner**
is admiral of this little land-fleet : he has control of
26 captains and **312 oxen.**   At a distance, the
white awnings of the wagons have **the** effect of a
fleet of vessels with all canvas spread.

  On 'leaving Leavenworth the drivers look well
enough, being all in new clothes, but as they advance into the plains, their good clothes become
travel-stained and torn, and at last are converted
into rags.   The *captains* have hardly proceeded
two hundred miles, before their trail is marked
with rags, scattered and flying along the **route.**
You may often remark also on the various **camping**
grounds, even as **far as the Rocky Mountains, and**
beyond, the wrecks of wagons and the **skeletons**
of oxen, but especially the remains **of** the wardrobe
of the traveller : legs of pantaloons and drawers, a
shirt-bosom, the back or the arm of a flannel vest,
stockings out at toe and heel, crownless hats, and
shoes worn through in the soles or uppers, are
strewed along the route.   These deserted camps
are **also** marked by packs of cards strewed **round**
among broken jars and bottles ; here you **see a**
gridiron, a coffee-pot, or a tin bowl ; **there a cooking-**
stove and the fragments of a **shaving-dish, all worn**
out and cast aside.   The poor Indians regard these

signs of encroaching civilization with an unquiet
eye as they pass them on their way. These rags
and refuse are to them the harbingers of the approach of a dismal future for themselves; they
announce to them that the plains and forests over
which they roam in the chase, their beautiful lakes
and rivers swarming with fish, and the repair of
numerous aquatic birds; the hearth which witnessed
their birth, and the soil which covers the ashes of
their fathers,—all, in fine, that is most dear to them,
—are about to pass into the hands of the rapacious
white man : and they, poor mortals, accustomed to
roam at large, and over a vast space, free like the
birds of the air, will be inclosed in narrow reserves,
far from their cherished hunting grounds and fine
fisheries, far from their fields of roots and fruits ; or
driven back into the mountains or to unknown
shores. It is not surprising, then, that the savage
seeks sometimes to revenge himself on the white
man; it is rarely, however, that he is the aggressor :
surely, not once out of ten provoking cases.

The wagons are formed every evening into a
corral. That is, the whole twenty-six are ranged in
a circle, and chained one to the other, so as to
leave only one opening, to give passage to the
beasts, which pass the night in the centre, and are
guarded there by several sentinels under arms.
Under the protection of a small number of determined men, the wagons and animals are secure

from any attack of undisciplined Indians, in however great numbers. When the travellers neglect
this precaution, and camp at random, not unfre-
quently a hostile band of Indians will provoke what
is called a *stampede*, or panic among the cattle, and
carry them all off at once. The travellers go into
camp early, and at break of day the beasts are let
loose in the prairie that they may have plenty of
time to graze. Grass is very abundant in the valley
of the Platte, and on the neighboring acclivities.

Between Fort Kearney and the crossing of the
South Fork of the Platte, we met over a hundred
families of Mormons on their way to Kansas and
Missouri, with the intention of settling there. They
appeared delighted at being fortunate enough to
leave, safe and sound, the famous promised land of
Utah; thanks to the influence of the new governor,
and the presence of the United States troops. They
told us that a great number of other families would
follow them, so soon as they should be capable of
doing so, and of procuring the necessary means for
the journey. They confessed that they would have
escaped long before, had they not been afraid of
falling into the hands of the Danites, or Destroying
Angels. These compose the body-guard of the
Prophet; they are said to be entirely and blindly
at his disposal, to carry out all his plans, meet all
his wishes, and execute all his measures, which
often involve robbery and murder. Before the

arrival of the United States soldiers, woe to any
one who manifested a desire to leave Utah, or
abandon the sect; woe to him who dared to raise a
voice against the actions of the Prophet,—they
rarely escaped the poniards of these Destroying
Angels, or rather incarnate demons.

The highway of the plains, during the beautiful
season of 1858, appeared, as it were, invaded by an
unusual and joyous animation. To complete the
idea which I have just given, I will add that couriers
and express messengers, coming and returning,
constantly crossed each other on the road. The
different companies of the army left a space of two
or three days' journey between them. Each company was followed by ambulances for the use of the
superior officers, a body of artillery and engineers,
and a train of wagons, with six mules each, transporting provisions and baggage. Each company
was followed also by an immense drove of six or
seven hundred horned cattle, to furnish their daily
food. Uncle Sam, as the Government of the United
States is called, has a truly paternal heart; he pro-
vides abundantly for the wants of the defenders of
the country, and will not suffer them to want their
comforts.

Every thing was going on admirably and in good
order. The commanding general and staff were
already at the crossing of the south branch of the
Platte, 480 miles from Fort Leavenworth, when he

received the news that the Mormons had submitted, or laid down their arms, and at the same time an order to distribute his troops to other points, and return to the United States. This also changed my destination; the conclusion of peace put an end to my little diplomatic mission to the Indian tribes of Utah. I consulted with the general, and accompanied him on his return to Leavenworth.

The South Fork of the Platte, at the crossing, is 2045 feet wide. In the month of July, its depth is generally about three feet, after the junction of the two forks, the width is about 3000 yards. The bottom, throughout the whole length, is sandy.

I could say much, dear Father, about the country between Leavenworth and the South Pass of the Platte, its botanical and other properties and productions, but I have spoken of these on many occasions in my letters describing other journeys across this region. The little incidents mentioned in this letter are all connected with my last trip.

Before leaving Fort Leavenworth for St. Louis, I made a little excursion of seventy miles to visit our dear Fathers and Brothers of the Mission of St. Mary among the Pottawatomies. I at last reached St. Louis in the beginning of September, after a first absence of about three months, and after a journey, to and fro, of 1976 miles. My stay in St. Louis was short. I will, in my next letter, give you details, which will inform you as to the particulars of the long expedition of which I speak in the first part of this letter.

Receive, Reverend and Dear Father, the expression of those sentiments of respect and affection which you know I entertain for you, and let me recommend myself very specially to your holy sacrifices and good prayers,

your Reverence's servant in Christ,

P. J. De Smet, S. J.

LETTER OF FATHER **DE** SMET.

St. Louis, Nov. 10, 1859.

Reverend and dear Father :

In accordance with my promise, I resume the
little story of my long voyage. On my return to
St. Louis, I tendered to the Minister of War my
resignation of the post of chaplain. It was not
accepted, because a new war had just broken out
against the Government, among the tribes of the
Rocky Mountains. I was notified by telegraph to
proceed to New York, and to embark there with
General Harney and his staff.

On the 20th of September, 1858, we left the port
of New York for Aspinwall; it was the season of
the equinox, so that we experienced some rough
weather in the voyage, and a heavy wind among
the Bahamas. We coasted for some time along
the eastern shore of Cuba, in sight of the promonto-
ries of St. Domingo and Jamaica. On the 29th I
crossed the Isthmus of Panama on a good railroad,
forty-seven miles long. The next day I had the
happiness to offer the holy sacrifice of the Mass in
the cathedral of Panama. The bishop very earnestly entreated me to use my influence with the Very
Reverend Father General at Rome, to obtain for

him a colony of Jesuits. His lordship especially expressed his earnest desire to intrust his ecclesiastical seminary to the care of the Society of Jesus. New Granada, as well as many other regions of Spanish South America, offers, doubtless, a vast field to the zeal of a large number of our Fathers.

The distance from Panama to San Francisco is more than three thousand miles. The steamer brought to in the superb bay of Acapulco to receive the mails, and to coal and water: this is a little port of Mexico. On the evening of the 16th of October, I arrived at San Francisco, happy to find myself in a house of the Society, and in the company of many of my brethren in Jesus Christ, who loaded me with kindness, and all the attention of the most cordial charity. The "*quam bonum et jucundum habitare fratres in unum*" is especially appreciated, when one leaves a California steamer in which one has been imprisoned, sometimes with fourteen or fifteen hundred individuals, all laboring under the gold fever, and who think and speak of nothing but mines of gold, and all the terrestrial delights which this gold is shortly to procure them. However, the " shortly" is long enough to allow of the destruction or disappearance of many an illusion. " All that glitters is not gold."

We left San Francisco on the 20th, and in a few days made more than one thousand miles to Fort Vancouver, on the Columbia river. The news of

the cessation of hostilities, and of the submission of
the tribes, had been received at Vancouver. **The**
task remained of removing the Indian prejudices,
soothing their inquietude and alarm, and correcting,
or rather refuting, the false rumors which **are** generally spread after a **war, and which,** otherwise,
might be the **cause** of its renewal.

Under the orders of the **general commanding** in
chief, I left Fort Vancouver on **the 29th of October,**
to go among the tribes **of the** mountains, at a
distance of about eight hundred miles. I visited
the Catholic soldiers of Forts Dalle City and Walla-
walla on my way. At the last-named fort, I had
the consolation of meeting Reverend F. **Congiato,**
on his return from his visit to the Missions, **and of**
receiving very **cheering news from** him **as to the**
disposition of the **Indians. At my request, the**
excellent **commandant of the fort had the very**
great kindness to set at liberty **all** the prisoners and
hostages, both Cœur-d'Alènes and Spokans, and
he intrusted to my charge **to** bring them on their
way, and return them to their respective nations.
These good Indians, particularly the Cœur-d'Alènes,
had given the greatest edification to the soldiers
during their captivity : these men often **approached**
them **with** admiration, in witnessing **the perform-**
ance of their pious exercises, **morning and evening,**
and in listening to their prayers and hymns. During the whole journey, these good Indians testified

the utmost gratitude to me, and their punctual performance of their religious duties was a source of great consolation and happiness to me.

On the 21st of November I arrived at the Mission of the Sacred Heart, among the Cœur-d'Alênes. I was detained at the Mission by the snow until the 18th of February, 1859. During this interval snow fell with more or less abundance for forty-three days and nights, on seven days it rained, we had twenty-one cloudy days, and sixteen days of clear and cold weather. I left the Mission on the 18th of February with the Reverend Father Joset, who accompanied me until we met Father Hoecken, who had promised to meet us on Clarke's River. The ice, snow, rain, and winds, impeded very much our course, in our frail canoes of bark, on the rivers and great lakes: we often ran considerable risk in crossing rapids and falls, of which Clarke's River is full. I counted thirty-four of these in seventy miles. We met with several camps of Indians in winter-quarters on every side. On the approach of the winter season, they are obliged to scatter in the forests and along the lakes and rivers, where they live by the chase and fishing. They received us everywhere with the greatest kindness, and, not-withstanding their extreme poverty, willingly shared with us their small rations and meagre provisions. They eagerly embraced the occasion to attend to their religious duties and other exercises of piety:

attending at the instructions with great attention, and with much zeal and fervor, at Mass, and at morning and evening prayers. On the 11th of March we arrived at the Mission of St. Ignatius, among the Pends-d'Oreilles of the mountains.

The Koetenays, a neighboring tribe to the Pends-d'Oreilles, having heard of my arrival, had travelled many days' journey through the snow to shake hands with me, to bid me welcome, and manifest their filial affection. In 1845 I had made some stay with them. I was the first priest who had announced to them the glad tidings of salvation, and I had baptized all their little children and a large number of adults. They came on this occasion, with a primitive simplicity, to assure me that they had remained faithful to prayer, that is, to religion, and all the good advice that they had received. All the Fathers spoke to me of these good Koetenays in the highest terms. Fraternal union, evangelic simplicity, innocence, and peace, still reign among them in full vigor. Their honesty is so great and so well known, that the trader leaves his store-house entirely, the door remaining unlocked often during his absence for weeks. The Indians go in and out, and help themselves to what they need, and settle with the trader on his return. He assured me himself, that in doing business with them in this style he never lost the value of a pin.

On the 18th of March I crossed deep snow a

distance of seventy miles, to St. Mary's valley, to revisit my first and ancient spiritual children of the mountains, the poor and abandoned Flatheads. They were greatly consoled on learning that Very Rev. Father General had the intention of causing the mission to be undertaken again. The principal chiefs assured me that since the departure of the Fathers, they had continued to assemble morning and evening for prayers, to ring the angelus at the accustomed hour, and to rest on Sunday, to glorify the holy day of our Lord. I will not enter into long details here, as to the present dispositions of this little tribe, for fear of being too long. Doubtless, in the absence of the missionaries, the enemy of souls has committed some ravages among them, but by the grace of God the evil is not irreparable. Their daily practices of piety, and the conferences I held with them during several days, have given me the consoling conviction that the faith is still maintained among the Flatheads, and still brings forth fruits of salvation among them,—their greatest chieftains, Michael, Adolphe, Ambrose, Moses, and others, are true and zealous Christians, and real piety in religion and true valor at war are united in them.

In my several visits to the stations in the Rocky Mountains, I was received by the Indians with every demonstration of sincere and filial joy. I think I may say that my presence among them has been of some advantage to them, both in a religious and secular point of view. I did my best to encourage them to persevere in piety, and to maintain the conditions of the treaty of peace with the Government. In these visits I had the happiness to baptize over a hundred infants, and a large number of adults.

On the 16th of April, in accordance with the orders of the commander-in-chief of the army, I went to Fort Vancouver, and left the Mission of St. Ignatius. At my request, all the chiefs of the different mountain tribes accompanied me, to renew the treaty of peace with the general and with the Superintendent of Indian Affairs; I give their names, and the nations to which they belonged. Alexander *Temglagketzin*, or the Man-without-a-horse, great chief of the Pends-d'Oreilles : Victor *Alamiken*, or the Happy-man (he deserves his name, for he is a saintly man), great chief of the Kalispels; Adolphus *Kwilkweschape*, or Red-feather, chief of the Flatheads; Francis *Saya*, or the Iroquois, another Flathead chief; Dennis *Zenemtietze*, or the Thunders-robe, chief of the Schuyelpi or Chaudières ; Andrew and Bonaventure, chiefs and braves among the Cœur-d'Alênes, or Skizoumish ; *Kamiakin*, great chief of the Yacomans ; and Gerry, great chief of the Spokans. The last two are still pagans, though their children have been baptized. We suffered much, and ran many dangers on the route, on account of the high stage of the rivers and the heavy snow. **For three** days we **had to** clear a way through thick forests, where thousands of trees, thrown down by storms, lay across one another, and were covered, four, six, and eight feet, **with** snow ; several horses perished in this dangerous passage. My horse stumbled many a time, and procured me many a fall; but aside from some **serious** bruises and scratches, a **hat** battered to pieces, a torn pair **of** trowsers, and a *soutane* or black-gown in rags, I came out of it safe and sound. I measured white cedars in the wood, which **were** as much as six or seven persons could clasp at the base, **and of** proportionate height. · After **a month's** journey, we arrived at Fort Vancouver.

On the 18th **of May** the interview took place with the general, the superintendent, and the Indian chiefs. It produced most happy results on both sides. About three weeks' time was accorded to the chiefs to visit, at the cost of Government, the **principal** cities and towns **of** the State **of** Oregon **and** Washington Territory, **with** every thing remarkable **in the way** of industrial establishments, steam-engines, forges, **manufactories,** and printing establishments,—of **all which the poor** Indians can **make** nothing or very little. The visit which appeared the most to interest the chiefs, was that which they made to the prison at Portland, and its wretched inmates, whom they found chained within its cells. They were particularly interested in the causes, motives, and duration of their imprisonment. Chief Alexander kept it in his mind. Immediately on his return to his camp at St. Ignatius Mission, he assembled his people, and related to them all the wonders of the whites, and especially the history of the prison. "We," said he, "have neither chains nor prisons; and for want of them, no doubt, a great number of us are wicked and have deaf ears. As chief, I am determined to do my duty : I shall take a whip to punish the wicked; let all those who have been guilty of any misdemeanor present themselves, I am ready." The known guilty parties were called upon by name, many presented themselves of their own accord, and all received a proportionate correction.

Before leaving the parts of civilization, all the chiefs received presents from the general and superintendent, and returned to their own country contented and happy, and well determined to keep at peace with the whites. As for me, I had accomplished among the Indians the task which the Government had imposed upon me. I explained to the general my motives for desiring to return to St. Louis by way of the interior. He acceded to my desire with the greatest affability, and in an answer which he addressed to me on this matter, he bore most honorable testimony to my services.

About the 15th of June, I again left Vancouver with the chiefs, to return to the mountains. I passed the 7th, 8th, and 9th of July at the Mission of the Sacred Heart, among the Cœur-d'Alênes. Thence, I continued my route for St. Ignatius with Father Congiato, and completed the trip in a week; not, however, without many privations, which deserve a short mention here.

Imagine thick, untrodden forests, strewn with thousands of trees thrown down by age and storms in every direction; where the path is scarcely visible, and is obstructed by barricades, which the horses are constantly compelled to leap, and which always endanger the riders. Two fine rivers, or rather great torrents,—the Cœur-d'Alêne and St. Francis Borgia,—traverse these forests in a most winding course; their beds are formed of enormous, detached masses of rock, and large slippery stones, rounded by the action of the water. The first of these torrents is crossed thirty-nine times, and the the second thirty-two times, by the only path; the water often comes to the horse's belly, and sometimes above the saddle. It is considered good luck to escape with only the legs wet. The two rivers are separated by a high mountain, or rather a chain of mountains, called the Bitter Root chain. The sides of these mountains, covered with thick cedar forests, and an immense variety of firs and pines, present great difficulties to the traveller, on account of the great number of trees which lie broken and fallen across the path, and completely cover the

soil. To these obstacles must be added immense
fields of snow, which have to be crossed, and which
are at times from eight to twelve feet deep. After
eight hours' painful march, we arrived at a beautiful plain enamelled with flowers, which formed
the summit of Mount Calvary, where a cross was
raised on my first passage, sixteen years ago. In
this beautiful situation, after so long and rude a
course, I desired to encamp; but Father Congiato,
persuaded that in two hours more we should reach
the foot of the mountain, induced us to continue the
march. When we had made the six miles which we
supposed we had before us, and twelve miles more,
darkness overtook us in the midst of difficulties. On
the eastern side of the mountain we found other
hills of snow to cross, other barricades of fallen
trees to scramble over; sometimes we were on the
edge of sheer precipices of rock, sometimes on a
slope almost perpendicular. The least false step
might precipitate us into the abyss. Without
guide, without path, in the most profound darkness,
separated one from the other, each calling for help
without being able either to give or to obtain the
least assistance, we fell again and again, we walked,
feeling our way with our hands, or crawled on all
fours, slipping or sliding down as best we could.
At last a gleam of hope arose; we heard the hoarse
murmur of water in the distance : it was the sound
of the waterfalls of the great stream which we were

seeking. Each one then directed his course towards
that point. We all had the good fortune to arrive
at the stream at last, but one after another, between
twelve and one o'clock in the night, after a march
of sixteen hours, fatigued and exhausted, our dresses
torn to rags, and covered with scratches and bruises,
but without serious injuries. While eating our
supper, each one amused his companions with the
history of his mishaps. Good Father Congiato ad-
mitted that he had made a mistake in his calculation,
and was the first to laugh heartily at his blunder.
Our poor horses found nothing to eat all night in
this miserable mountain gap.

I cannot omit here testifying my indebtedness to
all the Fathers and Brothers of the Missions of the
Sacred Heart and of St. Ignatius, for their truly
fraternal charity towards me, and the efficacious aid
which they rendered me towards fulfilling the special mission which had been intrusted to me.

As Father Congiato keeps the Very Reverend
Father General informed of the actual state of the
Missions of the mountains, it is unnecessary for me
to enter into all its details; I recommend, especially,
these poor children of the desert to his paternal
attention and charity, and to our immediate Supe-
riors in this country.

Divine Providence will not, I hope, abandon
them. They have already a great number of inter-
cessors in heaven, in the thousands of their children

dead shortly after baptism, in the number of good Christian adults among them, who, having lead good lives, have quitted this world in the most pious dispositions; they can especially count upon the protection of Louise, of the tribe of Cœur-d'Alènes, and of Loyola, chief of the Kalispels, whose lives were an uninterrupted series of acts of heroic virtue, and who died almost in the odor of sanctity.

On the 22d of July I left the Mission of St. Ignatius, accompanied by Father Congiato with some guides and Indian hunters. The distance to Fort Benton is about two hundred miles. The country for the first four days is picturesque, and presents no obstacle to travelling. It is a succession of forests easily traversed, of beautiful prairies, impetuous torrents, pretty rivulets; here and there are lakes, from three to six miles in circumference, whose waters are clear as crystal, well stored with fish of various kinds: nothing can be more charming than the prospect. We called one of the largest of these lakes, St. Mary.

On the 26th of July we crossed the mountain which separates the sources of the Clarke River from those of the Missouri, at the 48th degree of north latitude and the 115th of longitude. The crossing does not take more than half an hour, and is very easy even for wagons and carts. At the eastern base of the Rocky Mountains the plains are mountainous, and almost destitute of timber; we crossed several small streams before we reached the Sun River, and followed down its valley almost to its mouth. We visited the great falls of the Missouri on our way: the principal fall is ninety-three feet high. Father Hoecken and Brother Magri met us in this vicinity. On the 29th we arrived at Fort Benton, a post of the St. Louis Fur Company, where we received the greatest attention from all its inmates; we feel particularly obliged to Mr. Dorson, the superintendent of the fort, for his continued kindness and charity to all our missionaries. May the Lord protect and reward him! The Blackfeet occupy an immense territory in this neighborhood; they reckon from ten to twelve thousand souls in the six tribes which compose this nation. They have been asking for Black Gowns (priests) for many years, and their desire appears universal. In my visit to them in 1846, they begged me to send a Father to instruct them.

Father Hoecken is now in these parts, and I have just read with the greatest pleasure, in the "Annals of the Propagation of the Faith," that the work of the conversion of the Blackfeet has been commenced, with the entire approbation of the Very Reverend Father General.

On our arrival in the neighborhood, we found a large number of Indians encamped around and near the fort. It was the period for the annual distribution of presents. They manifested their joy at the presence of a missionary in their country, and hoped that "all would open to him their ears and heart." The chief of a large camp, in one of our visits, related to us a remarkable circumstance, which I think worthy of mention.

When Father Point was among the Blackfeet, he presented some crosses to many chiefs as marks of distinction, and explained to them their signification, exhorting them, when in danger, to invoke the Son of God, whose image they bore, and to place all their confidence in him. The chief who related these details, was one of a band of thirty Indians who went to war against the Crows. The Crows having got upon their trail, gathered together in haste and in great multitudes to fight and destroy them. They soon came up with them in a position of the forest where they had made a barricade of fallen trees and branches, and surrounded them, shouting ferociously the dreaded war-cry. The Blackfeet, considering the superior numbers of the enemy who thus surprised them, were firmly persuaded that they should perish at their hands. One of them bore on his breast the sign of salvation. He remembered the words of the Black Gown (Father Point), and reminded his companions of them; all shouted, "It is our only chance of safety." They then invoked the Son of God, and rushed from the barricade. The bearer of the cross, holding it up in his hand, led the way, followed by all the rest. The Crows discharged a shower of arrows and bullets at them, but no one was seriously injured. They all happily escaped. On concluding his statement, the chief added with energy and feeling: " Yes, the prayer (religion) of the Son of God is the only good and powerful one; we all desire to become worthy of it, and to adopt it."

My intention, when I left General Harney, was, with his consent, to go all the way to St. Louis on horseback, in the hope of meeting a large number of Indian tribes, especially the large and powerful tribe of Comanches. I was obliged to renounce this project, for my six horses were entirely worn out, and unfit for making so long a journey; they were all more or less saddle-galled, and, not being shod, their hoofs were worn in crossing the rocky bottoms of the rivers, and the rough, rocky mountain roads.

In this difficulty, I ordered a little skiff to be made at Fort Benton; worthy Mr. Dawson, superintendent of the Fur Company, had the very great kindness to procure me three oarsmen and a pilot. On the 5th of August I bade adieu to Fathers Congiato and Hoecken, and dear Brother Magri, and embarked on the Missouri, which is celebrated for dangers of navigation—snags and rapids being numerous in the upper river.

We descended the stream about 2400 miles in

our cockle-shell, making fifty, sixty, and sometimes, when the wind favored us, eighty miles a day. We took the first steamboat we met, at Omaha City. The steamer made about 700 miles in six days, and on the 23d of September, vigil of our Lady of Mercy, we entered the port of St. Louis.

During this long trip on the river we passed the nights in the open air, or under a little tent, often on sandbanks, to avoid the troublesome mosquitoes, or on the skirts of a plain, or in an untrodden thick forest. We often heard the howlings of the wolves; and the grunting of the grizzly bear, the king of animals in these parts, disturbed our sleep, but without alarming us. In the desert one perceives that God has implanted in the breast of the wild beasts the fear of man. In the desert, also, we are enabled in a particular way to admire and to thank that Divine Providence which watches with so much solicitude over his children. There is admirably verified the text of St. Matthew: "Consider the birds of the air, they sow not, but your Heavenly Father feeds them; are ye not of much more value than they." During the whole route, our wants were constantly supplied; yes, we lived in the midst of the greatest abundance. The rivers furnished us excellent fish, water-fowl, ducks, geese, and swans; the forests and plains gave us fruits and roots. We never wanted for game: we found everywhere either immense herds of buffaloes, or deer, antelope, **mountain sheep** or big-horns, pheasants, **wild** turkeys, and partridges.

On **the** way, along the Missouri, I met thousands of Indians of different tribes: Crows, Assiniboins, Minataries, Mandans, Rickaries, Sioux, &c. I always stopped a day or two with them. I received the greatest marks of respect and affection from these hitherto untutored children of the plains and mountains, and they listened to my words with the utmost attention. **For** many years these poor tribes have desired **to have** missionaries and **to be** instructed.

My **greatest,** I may say **almost** my **only** consolation, **is to have** been the instrument, in the hand of **Divine** Providence, of the eternal salvation of a great number of little children; of about nine hundred I baptized, many were sickly, and seemed only to wait for this happiness, to fly to God, to praise him for all eternity.

To God alone be all the glory ; **and to** the Blessed **Virgin Mary, our** most humble **and** most profound **thanks for the** protection and benefits received during **this long journey.** After having travelled, by land and river over 8314 miles, and 6950 on sea, without **any** serious accident, I arrived safe and sound **at St.** Louis, among my dear brethren in Jesus Christ. I am with the most sincere respect,

Your servant in Christ,

P. J. De Smet, S. J.

LETTER OF FATHER DE SMET.

St. Louis University, Dec. 1, 1861.

Dear Sir :

In my letter of **Nov. 10th, 1859, I** alluded to the Skalzi Indians. Allow me to add fuller details concerning that tribe.

I visited these good savages, for the first time, in the summer of 1845, on which occasion I had the happiness to regenerate all their little children in the holy waters of baptism, as well as a large **number of** adults. I saw these dear children **again in 1859 ; and** the visit **filled** me with inexpressible **joy,** because they had remained **faithful,—true** to the faith, and fervent and zealous Christians. They were the consolation **of** their missionaries, and shone conspicuous by their virtues among the tribes of the Rocky Mountains. They were especially distinguished by an admirable simplicity, a great charity, and a rare honesty in all their dealings with their neighbors, and an innocence of manners worthy of the primitive Christians. A short **account** of this interesting **tribe and the** country **which** they inhabit, will **doubtless please you.**

The **two** tribes of the Koetenays **and** Flat-bows number over a thousand souls. They are princi-

pally divided into two camps, and are known in
their country under the name of Skalzi. One of
these camps, numbering about three hundred, in-
habits sometimes the neighborhood of the great
Flathead Lake, and sometimes the great Tobacco
Plain, which is watered by the Kootenay River,—
the distance is about seventy miles. The Tobacco
Plain is a remarkable spot, situated between the
forty-ninth and fiftieth degrees of north latitude,
and is the only great plain possessed by this camp.
It is about fifty or sixty miles long, by fifteen or
twenty miles in width. It resembles a large basin,
surrounded by lofty mountains, which form a vast
and beautiful amphitheatre, and present a picturesque
sight. The plain has all the appearance of the dry
bed of a vast lake. Towards the south the valley is
gravelly, undulating, and covered with little hillocks,
and patches here and there are susceptible of cultivation; the northern portion, on the contrary, has a
uniform surface, and a considerable extent of excellent
arable land. Though the land is very elevated, and
far towards the north, the temperature is remarka-
bly mild, severe cold being a rare occurrence, and
the snow is seldom deep; it falls frequently during
the season, but disappears almost as it falls, absorbed,
perhaps, by the rarefaction of the atmosphere at this
elevation, or, perhaps, driven off by the southern
breeze, which blows almost uninterruptedly in the
valley, and drives the snow off as it falls. Horses

and horned cattle find abundant pasture during the whole year. The large river, called indifferently the Koetenay, the McGilvray, and the Flat-bow River, flows through the entire valley. It rises to the northwest of this region, and its course is towards the southeast for a considerable distance. The waters of this great river are increased by a large number of brooks and beautiful rivulets, which have their source, for the most part, in the lovely lakes or numerous basins of these beautiful mountains. Many of these streams present to the eye the most charming scenes in their course. The noise of their waters and the sweet murmur of their falls are heard at some distance, and the eye is charmed by their descent from height after height, and their succession of cascades, from which they escape to the plain, covered with foam, and, as it were, exhausted by the struggles of the way. These mountain torrents will some day be the sites of mills of every description. Coal exists in many portions of the country, lead is found in abundance, and I venture to say that more precious minerals repose in the bosom of the mountains, and will one day be brought to light there.

The Indians have devoted themselves to agriculture for some years past. They cultivate little fields of maize, barley, oats, and potatoes, all of which ripen. It is rare that the frost injures the crops before the season of harvest. Their small fields cannot be extended, owing to the want of instruments of agriculture. They are compelled to turn the earth with instruments of the most primitive construction, such as Adam may have used in his day. The pointed stick made of a very hard wood, is what they have used from ages immemorial to dig up the *camash*, the bitter-root, the *wappatoo* (*sagitta folia*), the *caious*, or biscuit-root, and other vegetables of the same description. These Indians are very industrious. They are rarely unemployed. Their time is fully occupied in making bows and arrows, lines and hooks, or in hunting and fishing, or seeking roots or wild fruits for their numerous families. They extend their hunt often to the great plains of the Blackfeet and the Crows, to the east of the Rocky Mountains, on the upper waters of the Missouri and the Sascatshawin. Deprived as they are of agricultural instruments and fire-arms, they are always in want, and they may be said to keep a perpetual Lent.

The missionaries furnished them with a few **ploughs and** spades. Last year I forwarded to them, **by** the steamer **of** the Missouri Fur Company **at St.** Louis, some necessary agricultural implements, such as ploughs, &c.; but the boat was burned with all her cargo above the Yellowstone river.

It is much to be regretted that no more can be done for these good Indians, for, of all the mountain tribes, they are at once the best disposed and the most necessitous. The beau-ideal of the Indian character, uncontaminated by contact with the whites, is found among them. What is most pleasing to the stranger, is to see their simplicity, united with sweetness and innocence, keep step with the most perfect dignity and modesty of deportment. The gross vices which dishonor the red man on the frontiers, are utterly unknown among them. They are honest to scrupulosity. The Hudson Bay Company, during the forty years that it has been trading in furs with them, has never been able to perceive that the smallest object had been stolen from them. The agent of the Company takes his furs down to Colville every Spring, and does not return before Autumn. During his absence, the store is confided to the care of an Indian, who trades in the name of the Company, and on the return of the agent, renders him a most exact account of his trust. I repeat here what I stated in a preceding letter, that the store often remains without any one to watch it, the door unlocked and unbolted, and the goods are never stolen. The Indians go in and out, help themselves to what they want, and always scrupulously leave in place of whatever article they take its exact value.

The following anecdote will serve to give an idea of the delicacy of conscience of these good Indians.

An old chief, poor and blind, came from a great distance, guided by his son, to consult the priest; his only object being to receive baptism, if he should be considered worthy of the privilege. He stated to the missionary, that, in spite of his ardent desire to be baptized, he had not dared to approach the priest for that purpose, owing to a small debt of two beaver skins (say ten dollars) which he had contracted. "My poverty," said he, "has always prevented me from fulfilling this obligation; and until I had done so, I dared not gratify the dearest wish of my heart. At last I had a thought. I begged my friends to be charitable to me. I am now in possession of a fine buffalo robe: I wish to make myself worthy of baptism." The missionary, accompanied by the old man, went to the clerk of the Company to learn the particulars of the debt. The clerk examined the books, but said that no such debt existed. The chief still insisted on paying, but the clerk refused to take the robe. "Have pity on me," at last exclaimed the worthy old man, "this debt has rendered me wretched long enough; for years it has weighed on my conscience. I wish to belong to the blameless and pure prayer (religion), and to make myself worthy of the name of a child of God. This buffalo robe *covers* my debt," and he spread it on the ground at the feet of the clerk. He received baptism, and returned home contented and happy.

10

A young Koetenay who had been baptized in infancy, during my first visit in 1845, had emigrated with his parents to the Soushwaps in the mountainous regions near Fraser River. His parents desired to marry him to a young woman who was as yet unbaptized ; he had a sister in the same condition. It was resolved that the three should make the long journey of many weeks' travel, to reach the Mission, in order that both sacraments might be received. On their arrival, their ardent faith, and praiseworthy earnestness, were the admiration of the whole village. The fervent missionary, Father Menetry, instructed these zealous neophytes, and prepared them for holy baptism. The young man, who had not seen a priest since 1845, had prepared himself to approach the tribunal of penance, for the first time, in order to make his first communion, and to receive the nuptial benediction with the proper dispositions. On the day appointed for the administration of all these sacraments, the young Koetenay presented himself with an humble and modest air at the confessional. He held in his hands some bundles of cedar chips, about the size of ordinary matches, and divided into small bunches of different sizes. After kneeling in the confessional and saying the confiteor, he handed the little bundles to the priest. "These, my father," said he, " are the result of my examination of conscience. This bundle is such a sin : count the chips and you will know how many times I have committed it; the second bundle is such a sin," and so he continued his confession. His confession was accompanied with such sincere signs of grief, that his confessor was affected to tears. It is impossible not to be struck with admiration for the simplicity of heart which led our young savage, in his desire to perform this duty with the utmost exactitude, to this new method of making a confession; but still more admirable is the adorable grace of the Holy Ghost, **who** thus sheds His gifts upon these, **His** poor children of the desert, and, if I may dare **to** say so, adapts himself to their capacity.

In their zeal and fervor the Koetenays have built a little church of round logs on the great Tobacco Prairie. They carried the logs,—which averaged from twenty to twenty-five feet in length,—in their arms a distance of more than a quarter of a mile, and raised the walls of the new church, as it were, by main force. The exterior is covered with straw **and sods.** In this humble house of the Lord they **meet morning and** evening, to offer to the Great Spirit **their** fervent prayers,—the first-fruits of the day. How striking is the contrast between this little church of the desert and the magnificent temples of civilization, especially in Europe. The majesty of these churches, their fine pictures, the sculpture which adorns their walls, and their imposing proportions, inspire the beholder with admiration and awe: yet, on entering this little **cabin**, consecrated to the Great Spirit in the desert, erected by poor Indians,—on contemplating the profound recollection, the sincere piety depicted on **their** features,—on hearing them recite their prayers, which seem to rise from the bottom of their heart, it is difficult to refrain from tears, and the spectator exclaims: " Indeed, this poor and humble church is the abode of the Lord and the house of prayer; its whole beauty lies in the piety, zeal, and fervor of those who enter there !"

In this humble church are now performed all the religious ceremonies of baptism and marriage. The Indians defer them until the appointed season for **the** arrival of the missionaries; they then come in from all parts of the country. " How beautiful are the feet of those who announce the Gospel of **peace.**" The priest of this Mission finds the truth **of the** words, "*Jugum meum suave:* my yoke is sweet." No sooner has he arrived than all crowd round him, as beloved children to greet, after a long absence, a father whom they tenderly venerate. Even the hands of infants are placed in those of the missionary by their mothers. A long conference then follows. The priest gives and receives **all** news of important events which have happened since the last meeting, and regulates with the chiefs the exercises to be followed during his present visit. He gives two instructions a day to adults, and catechises the children; he helps them to examine well their consciences, and to make a good confession: he prepares them to approach worthily the Holy Table, instructs the catechumens and admits them to baptism, together with the children born during his absence; he renews and blesses all new marriages; and, like a father, settles any difficulties which may have arisen. Some he encourages and strengthens in the Faith, and removes the doubts and soothes the inquietudes of others. In a word, he encourages all these good neophytes to know the Lord, to serve Him faithfully, and love Him with all their hearts.

If the days of the missionary are thus filled with labor and fatigue, he has his full recompense of merit and consolation. He counts them among the happiest days of his life. The Reverend Father Menetry, their missionary, during his visit in 1858, baptized fifty children and thirty adults, blessed forty marriages, and heard over five hundred confessions.

The great chief of the Koetenays, named Michael, recalls in the midst of his tribe the life and virtues of the ancient patriarchs. His life is that of a good and tender father, surrounded by a numerous family of docile and affectionate children. His camp numbers four hundred souls. They are all baptized, and they walk in the footsteps of their worthy chief. It is truly a delightful spectacle to find in the bosom

of these isolated mountains of the Columbia river,
a tribe of poor Indians living in the greatest purity
of manners, and leading a life of evangelic simplicity.
They are almost deprived of the succors of religion,
and receive the visit of a priest but once or twice
in the course of a year.

The sleep of a missionary among the Indians is
always deep. His entire day, and a great part of
the night, is spent in instructing them, and arran-
ging the affairs of their conscience. When his work
is done, his slumber is profound, and it is not surprising that he hears nothing that passes around
him. I wish to add, at this point, a little chapter
on the subject of Indian dogs. " *Experte crede
Roberto.*"

Having had much experience in this matter myself, I give ready and implicit faith to the statement
made to me by Father Menetry, as to the conduct
of the dogs of the Kootenays. It is the reverse side
of his beautiful description of life among this tribe.
All is not beauty and pleasure in this charming
wilderness. It is well that travellers at a distance
should be forewarned of what they may expect,
that they may provide themselves for the occasion.
If the traveller has only one tent, he must be careful before he retires to barricade the entrance well,
and surround it with brush; he must stop every
crack and cranny, and carefully hang out of reach
not only all his provisions, but any thing made of

leather, or that has **once had connection with** flesh, otherwise, he will find **on** waking, that himself and his cattle are deprived of provender. **The** Indian **dogs** are as bad as their masters are **good.** Their masters abhor theft, **but** these dogs **make it** their business, and subsist entirely by pilfering. The dogs are found to the number of six **or seven in** each family : each member owns one or **two ; they live on** bones and the crumbs which fall **from** the frugal table **of** their poor masters, and I can **assure you** that very **little** is left from the meal of an **Indian, who** considers it **a** duty to eat all that **is** set **before him, and** is by no means nice at table. The **dogs,** therefore, are left **to** provide for themselves **as best they can. For** the most part, they work **by** night, and become very cunning and expert : hunger sharpens their rapacious instincts. Father Menetry assures us, that he has very often awoke in the morning as poor as Job, every thing having been carried off during the night. It was **in vain** that he had taken **every** precaution which **prudence** suggested before going to bed, the industry **of these** nocturnal marauders got the better of all his care. **Sleeping** like a log after the fatigues of the **day, he** never heard the noise made by the thieves during their stay, though they often fought with one another in his tent over their spoils. The more vigilant savages were frequently aroused by the racket made in his tent, and were in the habit of coming to his rescue. Sometimes a good old Indian dame, armed with a big stick, would present herself suddenly upon the field of battle, dealing her blows right and left upon the combatants; again, a stalwart young savage would venture into the Father's tent to disperse these midnight marauders, and restore peace. Occasionally, the good Father himself would be aroused by the noise of the howling of the dogs and the cries of those who had come to protect him. They would then set to work to repair, though rather too late, the breaches made in his fortifications, stopping up every hole, and barricading the entry afresh. He would then lie down again, at the risk of another attack from these indefatigable robbers.

At last a council of chiefs was held on the subject, in which it was resolved to put an end to these scenes, so annoying to the missionary. They therefore surrounded his tent with an inclosure impenetrable to dogs. They went further, even, and set to work, in good earnest, to build a presbytery with two apartments, attached to the church. One room was made to serve for a sleeping-room, and the other to meet in, and for private conference with the priest. The good savages replaced, each time, the provisions and other objects stolen by their dogs. Taking the food as it were, from their own mouths and from those of their children, that the Father might not suffer from hunger; for fear that the want of necessaries might shorten his stay among them.

It appears from these little details, that **Charity**, the eldest daughter of Religion, flourishes in the soul of the simple savage, as well as in that of the children of Civilization. Though poorer and more humble among them, charity is not less industrious, not less beautiful: it is more simple and candid with them, and therefore more attractive.

P. J. DE SMET, S. J.

A VOCABULARY OF THE SKALZI,

OR KOETENAY TRIBE, INHABITING THE ROCKY MOUNTAINS ON THE HEADWATERS OF THE CLARKE AND MACGIL-VRAY RIVERS.

TAKEN DURING MY TRIP OF 1859.

Titto.	**Father.**
Kettitto.	My father.
Tittonis.	Thy father.
Tittowis.	His father.
Kittĕtōnelgle.	Our father.
Tittoniskelg.	**Your father.**
Galg.	Son.
Kannagalgli.	**My son.**
Galgtinis.	**Thy son.**
Galgliis.	His son.
Kannagenaggle.	**Our son.**
Galgniskilg.	**Your son.**
Kâkittĕgle.	My house.
Akitglênis.	Thy house.
Kakitglenègle.	Our house.
Akitgleniskilg.	Your house.
Koos.	**Pipe.**
Kakoosh.	**My pipe.**
Koosnish.	**Thy pipe.**
Koosish.	His pipe.

Kakooshnêglc.	Our pipe.
Akitsêmmelg.	Knife.
Kakessemmelg.	My knife.
Akessemmelgnis.	Thy knife.
Akessemmelgis.	His knife.
Kakkesemmelgnegle.	Our knife.
Joukisitnemme	Day.
Kitsilgmouiêt.	Night.
Sookĕne.	Good.
Tsênnin.	Bad.
Pekkêk.	Long ago.
Makke.	Soon.
Tittekête.	Man.
Tittekêtĕnintik.	Men.
Pelgki.	Woman.
Pelgkïmintik.	Women.
Nitstêhelg.	Young man.
Nitstêhelgnintik.	Young men.
Nutkwinne.	One.
Ash.	Two.
Kelgsê.	Three.
Gûtse.	Four.
Yikko.	Five.
Nmissê.	Six.
Wistelggle.	Seven.
Ogwātsê.	Eight.
Kykittŏwĕ.	Nine.
Ittŏwĕ.	Ten.
Ittowonglenkkwe.	Eleven.

Ittowongleäsh.	Twelve.
Ittowinnŏwe.	One hundred.
Ittowolg ittowinnowo.	One thousand.
Yŏwo.	**Twenty.**
Kattesennĕwe.	**Thirty.**
Gatsennŏwo.	Forty.
Jikunnĕwo.	Fifty.
Nmissennewo.	**Sixty.**
Westenenne.	**Girl.**
Egkomne.	**Infant.**
Kamma.	**Mother.**
Kennukglakkanelg.	My husband.
Kattelgnammo.	My wife.
Kessŭwi.	My daughter.
Kukkètŏgammelg.	My brother.
Kolgglitskilg.	My sister.
Akkĕsĕmākkănik.	**Indians.**
Ekkŏglêm.	**Head.**
Ekkuktĕglè.	**Hair.**
Akkakkăne.	Face.
Akkīnnĕkelg.	Forehead.
Akukkowête.	Ear.
Akakkĕglelg.	Eye.
Ako.	Nose.
Akelgmanna.	Mouth.
Welgglonêk.	Tongue.
Akonannê.	Teeth.
Akokkegleggê.	Beard.
Akokêk.	Neck.

Akëglêke.	Arm.
Aki.	Hand.
Akitskyhi.	Fingers.
Akukkĕpĕ.	Nails.
Akulgglêk.	Body.
Akkuksâke.	Leg.
Akkĕglik.	Foot.
Akilskakkămak.	Toes.
Makke.	Bone.
Akitglêwi.	Heart.
Wennĕme.	Blood.
Kikkĕglĕnām.	Village.
Nessōki.	Chief.
Kappilgglitit.	Warrior.
Kitsglêkilggla.	Friend.
Kitteglāna.	House.
Yēlskīme.	Kettle.
Kakĕglem.	My head.
Kakĕlglumma.	My throat.
Kakĕwettĕkêk.	My breast.
Kakenukkeglêke.	My stomach.
Kakĕwoom.	My belly.
Kakakkeglig.	My eyes.
Kaĉkkoon.	My nose.
Kakelglumma.	My lips.
Kowwelgglōnêk.	My tongue.
Kŭkkĕglêk.	My backbone.
Kaäkkĕsâke.	My legs.
Kajouskennek.	My knee.

Kaükkeglête.	My arm.
Kakĕgliek.	My foot.
Têwwo.	Gun, bow.
Akkĕ.	Arrow.
Akuttelg.	Axe.
Yakkĕsomelg.	Canoe.
Glenn.	Shoes.
Yakkyt.	Tobacco.
Ekkelglōmouët.	Sky.
Nettĕnnīkkĕ.	Sun.
Kítselgmittelgnukkăky.	Moon.
Akelgnōhōos.	Star.
Yokĕyitnēnnē.	Day.
Kilgmouit.	Night.
Nukkokĭgittĕnĕ.	Light.
Nêmmogonnê.	Darkness.
Woulgnêm.	Morning.
Glĕmāsït.	Spring.
Akkĕsōke.	Summer.
Suppĕnēkkoot.	Autumn.
Wennouït.	Winter.
Akkōmi.	Wind.
Numma.	Thunder.
Kelgglettelglig.	Lightning.
Akkeglukkekakkĕk.	Rain.
Akkĕglo.	Snow.
Kappĕkamākê.	Hail.
Akinnĕkukko.	Fire.
Woö.	Water.

Akowītc.	Icc.
Ammāk.	Land.
Akkelggleït.	River.
Akukkŏnōk.	Lake.
Akukglupgloït.	Valley.
Akŏwōgliït.	Mountain.
Akankammilg.	Island.
Nōki.	Stonc.
Kămĭskăglaggănĕ.	Salt.
Nilgko.	Iron.
Kakammŏgōmoolg.	Iloc.
Akăniggelg.	Powder.
Akkc.	Ball.
Akugglck.	Meat.
Kittckwakulggwa.	Flour.
Awomo.	Medicine.
Akenitsglaä.	Trcc.
Akukglekkopilg.	Leaf.
Akitssĕkelg.	Bark.
Sahelg.	Grass.
Gelgsi.	Dog.
Glukkŏpo.	Buffalo.
Nappĕko.	Black bear.
Kakki.	Wolf.
Suppĕky.	Decr.
Glôwwo.	Elk.
Sinna.	Beaver.
Akannukglam.	Snake.
Akkĕmakkê.	Egg.

Akkinnĕkäha.	Feathers.
Akowīte.	**Wings.**
Tiyakkegle.	**Duck.**
Egglêwĕ.	**Pigeon.**
Kiyakkeglo.	**Fish.**
Swakkämo.	Salmon.
Wiĕlg.	**Sturgeon.**
Kakikkeglit.	**My name.**
Kammĕnukkĕglo.	**White.**
Kennehoos.	**Red.**
Kamkokukkŏlg.	Black.
Kammakkĕsin.	**Yellow.**
Kakkegloyittĕky.	**Green.**
Kowilgky.	**Great.**
Kitssekunnê.	**Small.**
Kissemakkĕkê.	**Strong.**
Tilgnemme.	**Old.**
Kitssekunnê.	Young.
Kissook.	**Good.**
Kĕsähän.	**Bad.**
Kesahannelgkê.	**Ugly.**
Gettenukkĕn.	Alive.
Kiēp.	Dead.
Kiskéttegleït.	Cold.
Kuttemelggliït.	**Warm.**
Kammin.	**I.**
Ninko.	**Thou.**
Ninksish.	**He.**
Kammĕnelggle.	**We.**

Ninkŏmshkelg.	You.
Ninkoish.	**They.**
Tuno.	This.
Kappi.	All.
Yenakkenne.	**Many.**
Kelggle.	**Who.**
Akattêk.	**Near.**
Nŏw sinnemomtĕke.	To-day.
Walgkŏwa.	Yesterday.
Kannewouit.	To-morrow.
Hê.	Yes.
Māts.	**No.**
Woussilg **ikkĕne.**	**I eat.**
Woussilg ikougle.	I drink.
Wousnenglukkapekanne.	**I run.**
Wounowesgoume.	I sing.
Woutskomnêne.	I sleep.
Woulsisgenni.	I speak.
Onuppegonne.	I see.
Outsglekelnē.	I love.
Onēpilne.	I kill.
Onesakkenoune.	I sit.
Onewekene.	I stand.
Woutsnagge.	I go.
Oulsinglewīno.	I am angry.
Oultakatine.	I am lazy.
Oulsukkĕkokĭne.	I am glad.

INDIANS OF THE MISSOURI RIVER.

Omaha.	Otto.	Mandan.
1. Wiachtshe.	Yanki.	Niewâtza.
2. Nambah.	Nowê.	Nōpâ.
3. Thabĕnni.	Tani.	Nâwê.
4. Dabah.	Towê.	Tōpâ.
5. Satah.	Thatah.	Kiggou.
6. Phapê.	Schâkwe.	Ekkawa.
7. Penumba.	Schâmă.	Vhâpo.
8. Pélhabĕnni.	Grérabenni.	Nopapi.
9. Shanka.	Shumkê.	Niwatzâpie.
10. Grêba.	Krêpĕnnĕ.	Piaka.

Pawnee.	Rickarie.
1. Asko.	Achko.
2. Pipko.	Pipko.
3. Tàwit.	Tàwit.
4. Shititch.	Schêtilch.
5. Shiouks.	Schioug.
6. Shikshâpĕăch.	Schâpix.
7. Pikoushikshâpeah.	Schâpitsweêr.
8. Towikshâpeach.	Tawikshâpiesh.
9. Lookshiriwâr.	Loogshiriwâr.
10. Lookshirri.	Loógghent.

LETTER OF GENERAL HARNEY.

HEADQUARTERS, DEPARTMENT OF OREGON.
Fort Vancouver, W. T., June 1, 1859.

SIR :—I have the honor to report, for the information of the general-in-chief, the arrival at this place, on the 28th ultimo, of a deputation of Indian chiefs from the upper Pend-d'Oreilles, lower Pend-d'Oreilles, Flatheads, Spokans, Colville, and Cœur-d'Alêne Indians, on a visit, suggested by myself through the kind offices of the Reverend Father De Smet, who has been with these tribes the past winter, and has counselled them, both as an agent of the Government and in his clerical capacity, as to the advantages accruing to them by preserving peaceable and friendly relations with the whites at all times.

These chiefs have all declared to me the friendly desires which now animate them towards our people, and they assure me that their own several tribes are all anxiously awaiting their return, to confirm the peace and good-will they are hereafter determined to preserve and maintain. Two of these chiefs,—one of the upper Pend-d'Oreilles and the other of the Flatheads,—report that the proudest boast of their respective tribes, is the fact that no

white man's blood has ever been shed by any one
of either nation. This statement is substantiated
by Father De Smet. The chiefs of the other tribes
mentioned, state their people now regret they had
been so deceived and deluded as to go to war with
the whites the past year. They tender the most
earnest assurances that such will never be the case
again. All of these chiefs assert there will be no
difficulty for the future as regards the whites travelling through their country, or in the occupation
of it.

They request the Government to secure a reservation to their people, upon which they desire to
live and be protected.

Kamiakin, the noted chief of the Yakimas, came
in with these chiefs as far as Fort Walla-walla, with
the intention of surrendering himself to my custody,
but in consequence of an officious interference with
these Indians on the part of Mr. T——, agent for
the Flatheads, Kamiakin became alarmed, and returned to his people. No censure is to be attached
to Kamiakin for this act, and I have caused him to
be notified that I am satisfied with his present
peaceful intentions. . . . . .

I have also the honor to inclose a copy of Father
De Smet's report as to the Indian tribes he has
visited the past winter, which shows that peace
exists among themselves as well as with the whites;
and from my own observation I am convinced that

with proper care, another Indian war of any magnitude cannot soon occur in this department.

It gives me pleasure to commend to the general-in-chief the able and efficient services the Reverend Father De Smet has rendered.

I am, sir, very respectfully,
Your obedient servant,
W. S. HARNEY,
Brigadier-general commanding.

ASSISTANT ADJUTANT-GENERAL,
Headquarters of the Army, N. Y. City.

LETTER OF FATHER DE SMET.

FORT VANCOUVER, May 25, 1859.

DEAR CAPTAIN:

Towards the end of last March, owing to the deep snows and the impracticableness of the mountain passes, I received your kind favor of the 1st of January of the present year. I am happy to learn that my request to the general, about bringing down to Vancouver a deputation of the various chiefs of the upper tribes, met with his approval. I have no doubt, from the happy dispositions in which I left them at Walla-walla, the general's advice and counsel will be cheerfully and punctually followed out by them, and will prove highly beneficial to their respective tribes, and consolidate the peace established last fall by Colonel Wright.

During my stay among the Rocky Mountain Indians, in the long and dreary winter, from the 21st of November last until the end of April, I have carried out, as far as lay in my power, the instructions of the general. I succeeded, I think, in removing many doubts and prejudices against the intentions of the Government, and against the whites generally, which were lurking in the minds of a great number of the most influential Indians. I held frequent conversations with the chieftains of the Cœur-d'Alênes, the Spokans, several of the Shuyelpees, or Kettlefalls, and the lower Kalispels, who had chiefly aided, particularly the two first-mentioned tribes, in their lawless and savage attacks on Colonel Steptoe, and their war with Colonel Wright.

These various tribes, with the exception, perhaps, of a small portion of lawless Kettlefalls, *and lower Kalispels*, are well disposed, and will faithfully adhere to the conditions prescribed by Colonel Wright, and to any future requests and proposals of treaties coming from Government. The upper Pend-d'Oreilles, the Koetenays, and Flatheads, I found, as years ago, strong friends and adherents to the whites, and I have every reason to think that they will remain faithful; they ever glory, and truly, that not a drop of a white man's blood has ever been spilled by any one of their respective tribes. When I proposed to them that from each tribe a chief should accompany me down to Fort Vancouver, to pay their respects to the general, and to listen to his advice, all eagerly consented, and they kept in readiness for the long journey as soon as the snow would have sufficiently disappeared. Meanwhile, Major Owen, agent among the Flatheads, arrived at St. Ignatius' Mission, and made known to me that he had received orders from the Superintendent of Indian Affairs and **from** Commissioner Mix, to bring down to Salem **a chief** of each tribe of the upper country. Upon **this** declaration I persuaded the Indians that as Major Owen had received orders from the highest authority he superseded me, and they should **look** upon him as their leader in this expedition, while I would follow on with them, **as far** as practicable and I would be allowed. The major having brought **no** provisions for them, I lodged the chiefs in my own tent, and provided them with all necessary supplies from the 16th of April until the 13th instant, the day on which we reached Walla-walla, and where the chiefs were liberally provided for by **Captain** Dent, in command of the fort. The deputation of chiefs was stopped at Walla-walla by Major Owen, to await an express he had sent on from Spokan prairie, with instructions to the superintendent at Salem. My own instructions from the general, according to your letter of the 1st of January, "To return to Fort Vancouver as early in the spring as practicable, for some contingency might arise requiring the general's presence elsewhere," hurried me down in compliance with said order. With regard to Kamiakin, and his brother Schloom, I held several talks with them in February, March, and April, and acquainted them with the general's order, wish, and desire in their regard, namely, that they should follow me, and surrender into his hands, assuring them, in the general's own words, that "the Government is always generous to a fallen foe, though it is at the same time determined to protect its citizens in every part of its territory," &c. They invariably listened with attention and respect. Kamiakin made an open avowal of all he had done in his wars against the Government of the country, particularly in the attack on Colonel Steptoe, and in the war with Colonel Wright. Kamiakin stated that he strongly advised his people to the contrary, but was at last drawn into the contest by the most opprobrious language the deceitful Telgawax upbraided him with in full council, in presence of the various chiefs of the Cœurd'Alênes, Spokans, and Pelouses. Kamiakin repeatedly declared to me, and with the greatest apparent earnestness, that he never was a murderer; and, whenever he could, he restrained his people against all violent attacks on whites passing through the country. On my way down to Vancouver from St. Ignatius' Mission, I met him again, near Thompson's prairie, on Clarke's Fork. Kamiakin declared he would go down and follow me if he had a horse to ride, his own not being in a condition to undertake a long journey. · I had none to lend at that moment. At my arrival in the Spokan prairie, meeting with Gerry, one of the Spokan chiefs, I acquainted him with the circumstance, and entreated him, for the sake of Kamiakin and his

12

poor children, to send him a horse and an invitation to come on and to accompany the other chiefs to Walla-walla, and hence to Vancouver; it being his best opportunity to present himself before the general and superintendent, in order to expose his case to them and obtain rest and peace. Gerry complied with my request, and Kamiakin soon presented himself and joined the other chiefs. I had daily conversations with him until he reached Walla-walla : he places implicit confidence in the generosity of the general. I believe him sincere in his repeated declarations that henceforth nothing shall ever be able to withdraw him again from the path of peace, or, in his own words, "to unbury and raise the tomahawk against the whites." My candid impression is, should Kamiakin be allowed to return soon, pardoned and free, to his country, it will have the happiest and most salutary effect among the upper Indian tribes, and facilitate greatly all future transactions and views of Government in their regard. The Indians are anxiously awaiting the result, I pray that it may terminate favorably with Kamiakin. The sight of Kamiakin's children, the poverty and misery in which I found them plunged, drew abundant tears from my eyes. Kamiakin, the once powerful chieftain, who possessed thousands of horses and a large number of cattle, has lost all, and is now reduced to the most abject poverty. His brother Schloom, if he lives, will come in in the course of the summer. I left him at Clarke's Fork sickly and almost blind: he could only travel by small journeys. Telgawax, a Pelouse, I think is among the Buffalo Nez-Percés; from all I can learn, he has been the prime mover in all the late wars against Colonel Steptoe and Colonel Wright. His influence is not great, but he remains unceasing in his endeavors to create bitter feelings against the whites, whenever he can meet with an opportunity.

With the highest consideration of respect and esteem for our worthy general, and his assistant adjutant-general, I remain, dear Captain,

Your humble and obedient servant,

P. J. De Smet, S. J.,

Chaplain, U. S. A.

A. Pleasonton,
  Captain 2d Dragoons, A. Adjutant-general.

LETTER OF CAPTAIN PLEASONTON.

HEADQUARTERS, DEPARTMENT OF OREGON.
Fort Vancouver, W. T., June 1, 1859.

MY DEAR FATHER:

The general commanding instructs me to inclose a copy of his special order, No. 59, of this date, authorizing you to return to St. Louis through the different tribes of the interior, which you are so desirous to visit once again, for the purpose of confirming them in their good disposition towards the whites, as well as to renew their zeal and intelligence in the elements of Christianity,—the means so signally productive of good-will and confidence, in your labors of the past winter, requiring such self-denial and resolution.

On your arrival in St. Louis, the general desires you to report by letter to the adjutant-general at Washington, when your relations with the military service will cease, unless otherwise ordered by the War Department.

The general is anxious that I should communicate to you the deep regret with which he feels your separation from the service, and in making the announcement he is assured the same feeling extends to all those who have in any way been associated with you.

By the campaign of last summer submission had been conquered, but the embittered feelings of the two races, excited by war, still existed, and it remained for you to supply that which was wanting to the sword. It was necessary to exercise the strong faith which the red man possessed in your purity and holiness of character, to enable the general to evince successfully towards them the kind intentions of the Government, and to restore confidence and repose to their minds. This has been done : the victory is yours, and the general will take great pleasure in recording your services at the War Department; for such services no one feels more sensibly than yourself the proper acknowledgment is linked with the hopes that are cherished in the fulfilment of a Christian duty.

Satisfied that all necessary blessings will be bestowed upon you, in whatever sphere of duty you may be called to serve, the general will always be happy to tender to you the evidences of his esteem and friendship. I remain, Father, with the highest respect, Your most obedient servant,

A. PLEASONTON,

Captain 2d Dragoons, A. Adjt.-gen.

REV. P. J. DE SMET, S. J.,
  Chaplain, &c., Fort Vancouver, W. T.

12*

LETTER OF GENERAL HARNEY.

HEADQUARTERS, DEPARTMENT OF OREGON.
Fort Vancouver, W. T., June 3, 1859.

SIR:—I have the honor to inclose, for the information of the general-in-chief, an interesting report from the Rev. P. J. De Smet, describing the country of upper Washington Territory, in the vicinity of the Rocky Mountains, now occupied by various Indian tribes.

This report is valuable from the rare advantages Father De Smet possessed for many years, in his position as missionary among those tribes, to obtain accurate information of the country; and his purity of character will always give respect and importance to his statements.

The description he gives of the upper Clarke's Fork, the St. Mary's or Bitter Root valley, the valley of Hell's Gate Fork, the upper valleys on the headwaters of Beaver River, and the Koetenay country, in connection with his suggestion of collecting the remnants of the Indian tribes in Oregon and Washington Territories in that region upon a suitable reservation, is well worthy the serious consideration of the Government.

The country spoken of will not be occupied by

the whites for at least twenty years : it is difficult
of access, and does not offer the same inducements
to the settler that are everywhere presented to him
on the coast.

The system adopted in California of placing large
numbers of Indians upon a single reservation, and
causing them to adopt summarily the habits of life
of the whites, failed in consequence of the abrupt
transition brought to bear upon these simple and
suspicious people. The plan proposed by Father
De Smet is not open to this objection : it places the
Indians in a country abounding with game and fish,
with sufficient arable land to encourage them in its
gradual cultivation; and by the aid of the missionaries
at present with them, that confidence and influence
will be established over their minds, by degrees, as
will induce them to submit to the restraints of civilization, when the inevitable decree of time causes
it to pass over them.

From what I have observed of the Indian affairs
of this department, the missionaries among them
possess a power of the greatest consequence in their
proper government, and one which cannot be acquired by any other influence. They control the
Indian by training his superstitions and fears to
revere the religion they possess, by associating the
benefits they confer with the guardianship and protection of the Great Spirit of the whites. The
history of the Indian race on this continent has

shown that the missionary succeeded **where** the soldier and civilian have failed; it would be well for us to profit by the lessons its experience teaches, in an instance which offers so many advantages **to** the white as well as **to** the red man, and adopt the wise and humane suggestion of Father De Smet.

I am, sir, **very** respectfully,

Your most obedient **servant,**

W. S. HARNEY,

Brigadier-general commanding.

ASSISTANT ADJUTANT-GENERAL,
  Headquarters of the Army, N. Y. City.

LETTER OF FATHER DE SMET.

FORT VANCOUVER, **W. T.,** May 28, 1859.

DEAR CAPTAIN :

In compliance with the request of our worthy
brigadier-general, I herewith give you a short narrative of the upper Washington Territory, as yet
occupied by various Indian tribes, as far as my
views and observations may have extended during
several years' residence in that region, and particularly during the last winter trip I performed under
the special directions of the general.

The distance from Fort Walla-walla to the great
Spokan prairie, through which the Spokan River
flows, is about 150 miles. This whole region is
undulating and hilly, and though generally of a
light soil, it is covered with a rich and nutritious
grass, forming grazing fields where thousands of
cattle might be easily raised. It is almost destitute
of timber until you are within thirty miles of the
Spokan prairie, where you find open woods, and
clusters of trees scattered far and wide ; this portion,
particularly, contains a great number of lakes and
ponds, with ranges of long walls of large basaltic
columns, and beds of basalt. The country abounds
in nutritious roots (bitter-root, camash, &c.), on

which principally the Indians subsist for a great
portion of the year. The Spokan prairie is about
thirty miles from north to south, and from east to
west, bounded all around by well-wooded hills, and
mountains of easy access. The soil is generally
light, though covered with abundance of grass.

Along the base of the hills and the mountains
patches of several acres of rich arable land may
be found. The Spokan prairie is claimed by the
Cœur-d'Alêne Indians. Taking Cœur-d'Alêne Lake
as a central point, their country may extend fifty
miles to every point of the compass. The lake is a
beautiful sheet of clear water, embedded amid
lofty and high mountain bluffs, and shaded with a
variety of pines, firs, and cedars; in its whole
circumference, to my knowledge, there is no arable land. The low bottoms in several of its many
bays are subject to frequent and long inundations in the spring. The lake is about thirty miles
in extent from south to north, its width throughout
is from one to two or three miles. It receives its
waters principally from two beautiful rivers, the
St. Joseph and the Cœur-d'Alêne rivers, running
parallel from east to west; each is from sixty to
eighty yards broad, with a depth of from twenty to
thirty feet. After the spring freshet their currents
are smooth and even, and are hardly perceptible for
about thirty miles from their mouths, and until
they penetrate into the high mountain region which

separates their waters from those of Clarke's Fork
and of the St. Mary's or Bitter Root River; their
respective valleys are from one to three miles broad,
and are much subject to inundations in the spring;
the narrow strips of land which border the two
rivers are of the richest mould. The deep snows in
winter, the ice and water, keep these valleys literally
blocked up during several months (last winter it
continued for about five months). Small lakes, from
one to three miles in circumference, are numerous in
the two valleys. Camash, and other nutritious roots
and berries abound in them. Beautiful forests of
pine, &c., are found all along. The mountains bor-
dering the two valleys are generally of an oval shape,
and well wooded; a few only are snow-topped during
the greatest portion of the year. All the rivers and
rivulets in the Cœur-d'Alène country abound won-
derfully in mountain trout and other fish. The
forests are well stocked with deer, with black and
brown bears, and with a variety of fur-bearing animals. The long winters and deep snows must
retard the settlement of this country.

Clarke's Fork, at its crossing below the great
Kalispel Lake, is about forty miles distant from
Spokan prairie. Clarke's Fork is one of the principal tributaries of the upper Columbia. From its
entrance into the lake to the Niyoutzamin, or Ver-
milion River, a distance of about seventy miles, I
counted thirty-eight rapids. You meet with a suc-

cession of rapids and falls to its very head. Before it joins the Columbia, for a distance of about thirty miles, its rapids and falls are insuperable. In its whole length Clarke's River has few spots of good and arable soil, with ranges of dense and thick forests. The upper portion of the river, and its upper tributaries, have a succession of large prairies of light soil filled with water-worn pebbles, indicating bottoms or beds of ancient lakes. All these prairies are covered with a luxuriant and nutritious grass, and owing, probably, to the position of the high mountains by which they are surrounded, they are little or not covered with snows in the winter season. Such are Thompson's prairie, Horse prairie, Camash prairie, Jaco prairie, Flathead Lake prairie, with several other minor grazing fields. Far and wide apart, spots of less or more acres of good arable land are found; but too few, indeed, to make it for years to come, a thickly settled portion for the whites. The country of the upper Clarke's Fork, the St. Mary's or Bitter Root valley, the valley of Hell's Gate Fork, the upper valleys on the Beaver headwaters, the Kootenay country within the 49th degree, and under the jurisdiction of the United States, appear to be laid out and designed by Providence, to serve as reserves for the remnants of the various scattered tribes of Oregon and Washington territory, at least for some years to come. This region, I should think, might contain all the

Indians, and afford them the means of subsistence. The rivers could supply them with fish, the prairies with domestic cattle; deer and elk are still abundant, the buffalo grounds are not far off; wild edible roots and fruits are plenty; while in each section a sufficient portion of arable land might be found and reclaimed for their sustenance. Should all-the remnants of Indians be gathered in this upper region, one single military post would suffice to protect them against all encroachments and infringements of evil-disposed whites on Indians, and of Indians on the rights of the whites. As the reserves are now laid out in Washington and Oregon Territories, far and wide apart, surrounded and accessible on all sides by whites, experience teaches that it must lead to the speedy destruction of the poor Indians. Liquor and its concomitants, sickness and vice, will soon accomplish the work. Providence has intrusted and placed these weak tribes under the care and protection of a powerful government, whose noble end has always been to protect and advance them. If aided and assisted, in a proper situation, with agricultural implements, with schools, mills, blacksmiths, &c., I have no doubt but thousands of the aborigines might be reclaimed, and live to bless their benefactors. In the topographical memoir of Colonel Wright's campaign, recently published (page 75), I read to this effect: "The government, in its wisdom and prudence, should

13

make some timely provision for these many Indians by selecting for and placing them upon proper reservations, in order that they may not be caused to disappear by the fast-approaching **waves of civilization** and settlement, that must overtake and eventually destroy them." I have labored for several years among the **upper tribes in the** capacity of missionary. **My companions have carried on the** work to the present **time,** and will, **I** hope, continue their labors. The **want** of adequate means has greatly retarded one of the principal objects we had in view,—their civilization. We can all, and do, cheerfully testify to the good dispositions **of** these **upper tribes.** Should they be supplied **with the** necessary implements of agriculture, **with oxen, &c.,** they would **all work, and** would soon place themselves above want and in comfortable circumstances. As for schools, all are anxious **to** have their children taught. These are a few points I desire to be allowed to present to the consideration of the general, if they can in anywise tend to the amelioration of the lot of **Indians.** With the highest sentiments of respect and esteem, I remain, **Captain,** Your humble and obedient servant,

P. J. De Smet, S. J.,

Chaplain, &c., U. S. A.

A. Pleasonton,

Captain 2d Dragoons, A. Adjutant-general.

THE

SHORT INDIAN CATECHISM,

IN USE AMONG THE

FLATHEADS, KALISPELS, PENDS D'OREILLES,

AND OTHER ROCKY MOUNTAIN INDIANS.

INDIAN CATECHISM.

I.

Question. Tsŏst o kōlins, o êshtitestoms o jêtil gwa?

Answer. Tkolinzōtin o kokōlis o koeshtitestês.

Q. Gulstēm Tkolinzotin o kolins, gulstem o eshtitestoms?

A. Tkolinzotin kokolis o koeshtitestês gul ikssemipenōnum, gul iksgamenshum, gul ikysênwenem; tshci gul tik eppel ingwilgwilten takypshoi.

Q. Stem glo Kolinzotin?

A. Kolinzotin spagtpagt, tāpshoi, schiümlgest, essia eskolists, essia essowitsh.

Q. Gulstem koëszōti, Kolinzotin spagtpagt?

A. Netli Kolinzotin taop skeltitsh.

Q. Gulstem koëszoti Kolinzotin tāpshoi?

A. Netli Kolinzotin ta glo ĕlshei m ikskolis nêgŏ ta kypshoi.

Q. Gulstem koëszoti Kolinzotin schiümlgest?

A. Netli essia glo gest Lkolinzotin ĕltsi, essenshiitsin gest tel essia têstem.

Q. Gulstem koëszoti Kōlinzotin essia essowitsh?

INDIAN CATECHISM.

I.

Question. Who created **you** and preserves you to-day?

Answer. God created me and preserves me.

Q. **Why** did God create you, why does he preserve you?

A. **God** created me and preserves me, that I may know him, that I may love him, that I may obey him: **that so** I may have life without end.

Q. Who is God?

A. God is **a** spirit, without end, the best, omnipotent, all-seeing.

Q. **Why do** you say **that God is a spirit?**

A. **Because** God has no body.

Q. **Why do you say:** God is without end?

A. **Because there is no** time when God was born, because **he will have no end.**

Q. Why do you say: God is the best?

A. **Because** all good is in God, he is supremely good above all things.

Q. Why do you say that God sees all things?

13*

A. Netli Kolinzotin essowitch essıa jetilgwa, **glo** tle tgwêtsh, **nêgŏ** jêtillê glo **ëlshei, m kytssagêêl** nêgo glo nish shōt ky spoos.

Q. Lětien glo Kolinzotin?

A. Kolinzotin lstittshemaskyt **nêgō lessĕmilko** jêlestoleg.

II.

Q. A tsgwêwit **Kolinzotin?**

A. Ta, itshĕnaks glo Kolinzotin.

Q. A lsgwêgwit persones Lkolinzotin?

A. Onö, tshêtshêgles persones Lkolinzotin, Illêuw, Skousê, Saint Pagtpagt; shei essoustum Sainte Trinité.

Q. Stem glo Sainte Trinité?

A. Sainte Trinité etshĕnaks Kolinzotin **ltshêtshê-gles** persones.

Q. **Illêuw a** Kolinzotin?

A. Onē, Illêuw Kolinzotin.

Q. Skousê **a** Kolinzotin?

A. Onē, Skousê Kolinzotin.

Q. Saint Pagtpagt a Kolinzotin?

A. Onē, Saint Pagtpagt Kolinzotin.

Q. Illêuw, Skousê, Saint Pagtpagt, a tshêtshêgles Kolinzotin?

A. Ta; tshêtshêgles persones, pin itshenaks Kolinzotin.

Q. Gulstem tshêtshêgles persones o itshĕnaks Kolinzotin?

A. Because God sees all that is present, what is past, and what will happen hereafter, even the bottom of our hearts.

Q. Where is God?

A. God is in heaven and in all the earth.

II.

Q. Are there several gods?

A. No, there is but one God.

Q. Are there several persons in God?

A. Yes, there are three persons in God, the Father, the Son, and the Holy Ghost: this is called the Holy Trinity.

Q. What is the Holy Trinity?

A. The Holy Trinity is one God in three persons.

Q. Is the Father God?

A. Yes, the Father is God.

Q. Is the Son God?

A. Yes, the Son is God.

Q. Is the Holy Ghost God?

A. The Holy Ghost is God.

Q. Are the Father, Son, and Holy Ghost three gods?

A. No; three persons, but one God.

Q. Why are the three persons only one God?

A. Netli tshêtshêgles persones etsgägêêl l **cssia** têstem.

Q. Sŏwet tel tshêtshêgles persones glokoutôônt, glo shūti glo **yoyot?**

A. Ta; tshêtshêgles persones yoto etsgageel lessia têstem.

Q. Glo tshêtshêgles **persones a** estugtêgŭlum lsĕnils?

A. Onĕ, estugtegûlum lsĕnils, itshĕnaks tam **shci** itchenaks.

III.

Q. A itshenaks tel tshêtshêgles persones kolist schyloug?

A. Onĕ, itshenaks kolist schyloug.

Q. Sowet tel ltshêtshêgles persones kolist schyloug?

A. Kolinzotin Skousê.

Q. Etie etsägeel Kolinzotin **Skousê kolist schy-**loug?

A. Kolinzotin Skousê kolist schyloug, kwyst skeltitsh, a singappêus etsägeel je kampîle.

Q. Tel letien Kolinzotin Skousê kwyst skeltitsh o singappeus?

A. Kolinzotin Skousê kwyst skeltitsh o singappeus tel snitelses stêtshĕmish Mary, olkshīlum Saint Pagtpagt.

Q. **Kolinzotin** Skousê kolist schyloug, **a hoi** Kolinzotin?

A. Ta, Kolinzotin Skousê yettilgwa Kolinzotin nêgŏ schyloug.

A. Because the three persons are equal in all things.

Q. Which of the three persons is the great, old, powerful?

A. No, the three persons are equal in all things.

Q. Do the three persons differ from each other?

A. Yes, they differ; one is not the other.

III.

Q. Did one of the three persons become man?

A. **Yes, one of them became man.**

Q. Which of the three persons became man?

A. The Son of God.

Q. How did the Son of God become man?

A. The Son of God became man, he took a body and soul like us.

Q. Whence did the Son of God take his body and soul?

A. The Son of God took his body and soul from the womb of the Virgin Mary, by the operation of the Holy Ghost.

Q. Did the Son of God, become man, cease to be God?

A. No, the Son of God is now God and man.

Q. Gulstem Kolinzotin Skousê kolist schyloug?

A. Kolinzotin Skousê kolist schyloug, gul kakyin nylgglis glo tel tyje, gul kakysgwitsils kakel ingwil-gwilsenta kaypshoi.

Q. Sowet glo skests Kolinzotin Skousê, kolist schyloug?

A. Kolinzotin Skousê kolist schyloug, Jesus Christ glo skwests.

Q. Sowet Jesus Christ?

A. Jesus Christ Kolinzotin Skousê kolist **schy-**loug.

Q. Letien etsägeel Tjesus Christ o ky in nyglis?

A. Jesus Christ kyinnyglglis sttlils, gul kampïlĕ lessyïmeus.

Q. Jesus Christ a eltsi glo ltumtumny?

A. Jesus Christ eltelschyloug tshatelkatilsh **glo telslil.**

Q. Jesus Christ glo eltelschy**loug kassip a sïllĕ** jelestolig?

A. Ta, mousselopenstaskyt glo tel eltelschylong o elnuwisk schillis esteltshemāskyt.

Q. Nam elsgoui jelestolig?

A. Onē, Jesus Christ nem elsgoui jelestolig, l ets eûwit schalgalt, iks innemiêpĕlems glo esgwilgwilt, glo estlil.

Q. Stem glo iks innemiêpĕlems kyjelemigom Jesus Christ?

A. Nem gwiyousis glo gest lstittshemaskyt, nêm gwêlst glokwaökōt lessoliep.

Q. Why did the Son of God become man?

A. The Son of God became man to redeem us from evil, to give us life without end.

Q. How is the Son of God, become man, called?

A. The Son of God, become man, is called Jesus Christ..

Q. Who is Jesus Christ?

A. Jesus Christ is the Son of God, made man.

Q. How did Jesus Christ redeem us?

A. Jesus Christ redeemed us because he died on the Cross for us.

Q. Did Jesus Christ remain among the dead?

A. Jesus Christ came to life on the third day after his death.

Q. Did Jesus Christ remain long here on earth after he came to life again?

A. No; forty days after he came to life again, he ascended to heaven.

Q. Will he return to the earth?

A. Yes, Jesus Christ will return to the earth on the last day, to judge the living and the dead.

Q. What will our Lord Jesus Christ judge?

A. He will take the good to heaven, he will cast the wicked into a place of fire.

IV.

Q. Lsowet Jesus Christ ltekwintês **glo ky** semyltums glo skolkwelts, glo tshy ikssemiäkeltums lstittshemaskyt?

A. Jesus Christ tekwintês l onêgŏ miĕnsotin l ntshaumin.

Q. Stem glo Sintshaumin?

A. Sintshaumin essia glo tshy essenoningwênemsh nêgŏ esseuwĕnemst Jesus Christ innemitsinsōtis.

Q. Sowet glo onêgo Jesus Christ innemitsinsotis?

A. Esanrostum Pape, evêque, nêgŏ kwailoks.

Q. A gwiet glo Sintshaumin?

A. Ta, inko glo onêgo Sintshaumis Jesus Christ, ishy onego ingwilgwiltin.

Q. Lêtien **glo onègo Sintshaumin**?

A. Sintshaumin Catholique, Apostolique, **Romaine, shy glo** onêgo Sintshaumis Jesus Christ.

Q. Sowet o jelemigums Siņtshaumin Jesus Christ?

A. Jesus Christ jelemigum ta kysewîtshtum. Pape jelemigum kysewitshstum.

Q. Sintshaumin pentitsh a essonêgwi glo lkysemyellills?

A. Onē, netli pentitsh estoggŏmim t Saint **Pagtpagt.**

Q. Letien glo tyje, glo tshy o ta esseuwnemist Sintshaumin Jesus Christ nêgo glo innemitsinsotis?

IV.

Q. To whom did Jesus. Christ commit to teach what he said, to show the way of heaven?

A. Jesus Christ committed it to the true teachers of his Church.

Q. What is the Church?

A. The Church is all who believe and obey the interpreters of Jesus Christ.

Q. Who are the true interpreters of Jesus Christ?

A. They are called Pope, bishop, and priest.

Q. Are there more churches than one?

A. No, there is one true Church of Jesus Christ: in it alone is life everlasting.

Q. Where is the true Church?

A. The Catholic, Apostolic, Roman Church, that is the true Church of Jesus Christ.

Q. Who is the head of the Church of Jesus Christ?

A. Jesus Christ is the head that we see not, the Pope is the head that we see.

Q. Does the Church always speak truly in what it teaches us?

A. Yes, because the Holy Ghost always directs it.

Q. What sin does he commit who does not obey the Church of Jesus Christ and his interpreters?

A. Shy glo ingoutgoutsin, glo sinshiïtemissotin : shy glo ky auwstum heretique : tshy esgwioustum lessoliep.

.V.

Q. Letien m'etsageel glo kykelsōt in kygwilgwilt lstittshemaskyt?

A. Kakysagēli tgest schosigults Kolinzotin.

Q. Sowet glo gest schosigults Kolinzotin?

A. Glo shy eppel baptême, nêgŏ essenoningwè- nemists nêgŏ essenwenêmists skolkwelts Kolinzotin.

Q. Letien glo kaksenoningwênêmĭn?

A. Shy je ky auwauwstum ltshaumin Noningwe- nêmin Lkolinzotin Illeuw, etc.

Q. Auwst glo shy ntshaumin.

A. Noningwenemin Lkolinzotin Illeuw, etc.

Q. A esse noningwenemstoug glo shy ntshaumin?

A. Onē, noningwenemin, netli Kolinzotin kog- witsl glosnoningwènetin tel baptême.

VI.

Q. Lstem o kysougstum glo schosigults Kolin- zotin?

A. Lstakkatakkensout essyimeus.

Q. Letien m etsageel glo kōkostakketakkensout essyimeus?

A. Tĕkanten istliltshemêshin, tel shy lissemilshe- mêlis, tel shy lisshēzikwe lissintshummelkyt, tel shy listshishêtsh : O tson lskwests Illeuw, o Skousê, o Saint Pagtpagt.   Komi etsageel.

A. The sin of arrogance, pride, which is called heresy : this leads to fire.

V.

Q. What must we be to live in heaven?

A. We must act as good children of God.

Q. Who is a good child of God?

A. He who is baptized, and believes and obeys the word of God.

Q. Where is what we are to believe?

A. What we say in the prayer : "I believe in God the Father," &c.

Q. Say this prayer.

A. I believe in God the Father, &c.

Q. Do you believe this prayer?

A. Yes ; I believe, because God gave me faith in baptism.

VI.

Q. By what do we know the children of God?

A. By the making of the sign of the Cross.

Q. How must we make the sign of the Cross?

A. I sign the forehead, then the breast, then the left shoulder, then the right, and say : "In the name of the Father, and of the Son, and of the Holy Ghost. Amen."

Q. Stem glo kysinkukkekomme glolis tstakketak kensout essyimeus?

A. Kysinkukkekommeglolis Sainte **Trinité nêgŏ** glo tlil Jesus Christ essyimeus.

Q. Letien o etsägeel kysinkukkekomeglolils **Sainte** Trinité?

A. Glo ky auwauw Illeuw, Skousê, o **Saint Pagt-pagt.**

Q. Letien o etsageel kysinkukkekomeglolils glo stlils Jesus Christ?

A. Gul ky yimeuslum lkampĭle glo eshy tlil Jesus Christ.

Q. Pĭstêm m kystak ketakkensout essyimeus?

A. Agal kakstshaum, nêgŏ glo têstem kykskolintum, nêgŏ glo kykopillelt kykskwentum glo **tyje.**

Q. Gulstem o kystakketakkensout **agal kykst-shaum,** nêgŏ testem kykskolintum?

A. **Ky** gwitseltum Lkolinzotin, kyksolkschitlils tsĕnils, gest **kykskolum.**

Q. Gulstem kykstakketakkensout, agal glo kykopillilt kykskwentum tyje?

A. Kaksgalittestum kaksolkschitlils ta kykskwen-**tum** glo tyje.

VII.

Q. 'Letien o kyksauro auwstum glo kyksseuwene?

A. Lntshaumin: shy glo ko Anjelemigum Koankolinzotin keije, etc.

Q. What must we remember when we make the sign of the Cross?

A. We must remember the Blessed Trinity, and that Jesus Christ died on the Cross.

Q. How are we to remember the Holy Trinity?

A. Because we name the Father, Son, and Holy Ghost.

Q. How do we remember the death of Jesus Christ?

A. Because we form on ourselves the Cross on which Jesus Christ died.

Q. When must we make the sign of the Cross?

A. Always when we pray and when we do any thing, and when we are incited to do any evil.

Q. Why do we make the Cross before we pray or do any thing?

A. We give them to God, that we may be helped by God to do them well.

Q. Why do we make the Cross when we are incited to do any evil?

A. We ask to be helped not to do evil.

VII.

Q. Where do we say the things that we are to do?

A. In the prayer: "I am the Lord thy God," &c.

14*

Q. Letien o etsageel kykelsotin glo kakyseuwenistumglië skolkwelts?

A. Kakysgĕmenshum glo Kolinzotin tessemilko kyspoös nêgŏ kaksgemenshum kysinnukshyloug, etsageel kampile.

Q. A nêgŏ **kakyseuwene** glo **skolkwelts Sint**-shaumin?

A. **Onē, netli** Tkolinzotin kytsotsils.

Q. Auwauwt glo skolkwelts Sintshaumin.

A. Akysseuwene koetoont stshaum.

VIII.

Q. Ko nām ky elkonten glo i tkaimpile **kykseu**-wene glo skolkwelts Kolinzotin?

A. **Ta,** kakyksolkshitlels Tkolinzotin.

Q. Letien o m etsageel glo kykelsōt um kyksolk-shitlils Tkolinzotin?

A. Kakystshauwi kakyskomen Sacrements.

Q. Stem glo shiumlgest tel essia nstshaumin?

A. Shy tky jilemigom Jesus Christ kymyellils.

Q. Auwnt **glo** shy ntshaumin.

A. Kyleuw lstittshemaskyt, etc.

Q. **Stem** glo ksesselils ntshaumin glo kakyse-mium?

A. Sinkintistis l'ange, tshy kyskolkwelstum **glo** stĕtshĕmish **Maly,** skois Jesus **Christ.**

Q. Auwt glo sinkuitistis **l'ange.**

A. Tshinkuitis Maly, etc.

Q. How must we act to do **as** this says?

A. We must love God with all our heart, and we must love our neighbor as ourselves.

Q. Must we also do what the Church says?

A. Yes, because God tells us so.

Q. Name what the Church says.

A. Hear the great prayer.

VIII.

Q. Are we able alone (of ourselves) to do **what** God commands?

A. No, we must be helped by God.

Q. What must we do to be helped by God?

A. We must pray and receive the Sacraments.

Q. Which is the best among all prayers?

A. That which our Lord Jesus Christ teaches us. .

Q. Recite that prayer.

A. Our Father in heaven, &c.

Q. What **is** the second prayer which we must know?

A. The salutation of the angel, and in it we speak to the Virgin Mary, mother of Jesus Christ.

Q. Recite the angelic salutation.

A. I salute thee (*i. e.*, Hail), Mary, &c.

IX.

Q. Stem glo tyje?

A. Tyje, glo ta kyseuwenemtum glo skolkwelts Kolinzotin.

Q. Kwinish estugtēgūlum glo tyje?

A. Esseltoleg : inko glo tyje lkyspoos, estōko i kykolil o glo inkoleg tkampīle o kykwentum.

Q. Stem glo tyje lkyspoos estoko i kykolil?

A. Shy glo kwyst tyje kyleuw Adam gul ta seuwenêmis Kolinzotin.

Q. Pistem tkampile m ky kwentum glo tyje?

A. Ne kystikkitsog ta kyseuwenemintum glo Kolinzotin.

Q. Kwintsoleg estugtegulem glo tyje, kykwestum tkampile?

A. Esselloleg, inko ntliltien, inko tam ntliltien.

Q. Stem glo ntliltien tyje?

A. Gulshy o kygwellils Tkykolinzotin, nêgŏ okyshimgelils Tkykolinzotin, nêgŏ tshy kysgwienlils lessoliep.

Q. Gul kwinish ntliltien tyje m kygou tssoliep?

A. Gul inko, ne ta kyelkolgwêlils um kytlil.

Q. Stem glo, tām ntliltien, tyje?

A. Tshy o geel, ta kysolkshitlils Tkykolinzotin.

Q. Lkwinshsoleg o kyskwestum glo tyje?

IX.

Q. What is evil (sin)?

A. It is evil not to do what God says.

Q. How many kinds of evil are there?

A. Two; one (original sin) is in our hearts when we are born, one that we do ourselves.

Q. What is the evil that is in our heart when we are born?

A. That which Adam our Father took because he did not do what God said.

Q. When do we ourselves do evil?

A. When of our own accord we do not hear God.

Q. Of how many kinds is the evil we do ourselves?

A. Of two kinds, one giving death, one not giving death.

Q. What is the evil giving death?

A. For this we are rejected by God, we are enemies of God, he casts us away into hell.

Q. For how many mortal sins shall we go to hell?

A. For one, if it is not forgiven before we die.

Q. What is the sin not giving death?

A. That which makes us to be less assisted by God.

Q. In how many ways do we do evil?

A. Lsilkstoleg : tky inpoostin, tky inkomtsintin, tky inkolkweltin, tky skeltitsh, tky sinnouwilsêmen.

Q. Kwinĭsh glo essinshiitsin tyje ?

A. Sispel : sinshiitsemiṣsotin, siyokwe, tshêtshêt tyje, intshegoutleslin, sintellane, snaiëmils, snowylis.

X.

Q. Stem glo Sacrement ?

A. Sacrements Jesus Christ tskolist etsageel maliëmmisten lkysingappeus.

Q. Kwinish glo Sacrements ?

A. Sispel : Baptême, Injojotillistin, Eucharistie, Sinnemipemist, Sacrement Lessemiogti, Sinkwail-okstin, Singonnogweus.

Q. Stem glo Baptême ?

A. Tshy o kykolgwêllis glo tyje, lkyspoos o estoko o kykolis. Nêgŏ kyschousigultlils Tkolinzo-tin nêgŏ Tsinshanmin.

Q. Stem glo Injojotillistin ?

A. Tshy o kygwilsils Saint Pagtpagt, kysolkshi-tlils kakgesti shousigults Kolinzotin.

Q. Stem Eucharistie ?

A. Eucharistie shy onêgo skeltits, singôls, singap-peus kyjilemigom Jesus Christ, je létsägeel etsgwako.

Q. Stem glo Sinnemipemist ?

A. Tshy kyelkolgwêlils glo tyje kyskwestum tel kywisle baptême lils.

Q. Stem Sacrement glo Lessemiogti ?

A. In five ways: in our heart, in desire, in speech, in body, by sloth.

Q. How many sovereign (deadly) sins are there?

A. Seven: pride, avarice, the foul sin, anger, gluttony, envy, sloth.

X.

Q. What is a Sacrament?

A. Jesus Christ instituted the Sacraments as medicines of the soul.

Q. How many Sacraments are there?

A. Seven: Baptism, Confirmation, the Eucharist, Confession, the Sacrament of those grievously sick, Order, Matrimony.

Q. What is Baptism?

A. By this is remitted the sin that is in our heart when we are born. By it we are made children of God and of the Church.

Q. What is Confirmation?

A. By it is given to us the Holy Ghost, we are helped to be good children of God.

Q. What is the Eucharist?

A. The Eucharist, truly the body, blood, soul of our Lord Jesus Christ, although as it were under flour.

Q. What is Confession?

A. By it are remitted the sins which we have committed since we were baptized.

Q. What is Extreme Unction?

A. Tshy o essolkshitum glo essemiogti skollits o singappeus.

Q. Stem glo Sinkwailokstin?

A. Tshy o eskolil akkelinnemitsinsolis **Jesus** Christ.

Q. Stem glo Singonnogweus?

A. Tshy o eskōlstum aktshissinnewêgo **glo** skaltemig **o semcêm** etsageel schousigults **Kolinzotin.**

XI.

Q. Stem glo Sinnemipemist?

A. Sinnemipemist glo kysglakommistên essia glo tyje kyskwen Ikwailaks kakykēlkolgwêllils.

Q. Etien **o** etsageel **um** gest kymipemish?

A. **1. Kaksinko**lkolsinsotum glo **tyje kyskwen.**

2. Kakyspōpōsensh.

3. Kakstsogschitum **ta kakēlkwentum glo tyje.**

4. Kaksglakommisten **glo tyje; ta** kakeppel **wékwintum.**

Q. Etien glo tyje glo kyksinkolk**olinsotum**?

A. Glo tyje kyskwen tky impoostis, tky inkamsinlin, **tky** inkolkwenten, tky skeltils, tky snonyllis: kyksmkolkolsinsotum glo skolkwelts Kolinzotin nêgŏ Sintshaumin.

Q. Agest glo sinnemipemists glo tagest **essin**kolkolsintotums?

A. Ta.

Q. Agest glo sinnemipemists **glo** essêwékwest **intliltien tyje?**

A. It helps those grievously sick in soul and body.

Q. What is Order (the making of Black Gowns)?

A. Thereby one becomes a minister of Jesus Christ.

Q. What is Matrimony?

A. This unites a man and woman as children of God.

XI.

Q. What is Confession?

A. We manifest all evil deeds to the priest to be remitted.

Q. How shall we confess well?

A. 1. Our bad deeds are to be recalled to mind.

2. We must repent.

3. We must resolve not to do evil any more.

4. We must manifest our sins, we must conceal none.

Q. What evil must we call to mind?

A. Evil done in our heart, in desire, speech, body, by sloth : we must be mindful of the commands of God and of the Church.

Q. Does one confess well who does not call to mind?

A. No.

Q. Does one confess well who conceals a mortal sin?

A. Ta, stittegwintês glo tle skwys tyje.

Q. Letien m kyŝagelum glo kaksemipemist?
A. 1. Kakyssensilloggwêpi.
2. Mkakstakketakkeus **sout,** um kytsōntum kwin :
Illeuw ko tshauwst **netli** kwen tyje.
3. Kwemt ky myeltum glo lshy o etsageel glo
kys kwen glo tyje.
Q. Letien m **kysagelum glo neky** wissemyeltum
glo **tyje?**
A. 1. Kakyspopoosentsh.
2. Kakysseuwenem glo tkwenloks kytsōtlils.
3. Ta kyks stēgulumstum glo neky seuwenum-
tlils.
Q. Letien m kysagelum ne kywissemipemist?
A. 1. Kakselemtem glo Kolinzotin.
2. Kakysauwauwin ntshaumin, **kystsotlils tkwai-
loks.**

XII.

Q. Stem glo Sinkytsinum?
A. Sinkytsinum kykwentūm glo skeltits, glo
singols, glo singappeus Jesus Christ kyjilemigom.
Q. Akaky skamtsinum glo Tsinkytsinum?
A. Onē, gul kootōnt skolis lkampile.
Q. Stem glo skolis Sinkytsinum?
A. 1. Kys **clousils Ljesus Christ.**
2. Tshy o kykōllis geel taksjojot kyspoos ltyje.
3. Telsi kyksgestilisshy.

A. No, he adds another sin to those already committed.

Q. How must we confess?

A. 1. We kneel down.

2. We make the sign of the Cross, and say: "Father, pray for me, because I have done evil."

3. Then we manifest how we have done evil things.

Q. How must we behave after we manifest **our** sins?

A. 1. We must be sad.

2. **We must listen** to **what is** said by the **priest.**

3. We must not change any thing if **we are** questioned.

Q. How must we do after confession?

A. 1. We must return thanks to God.

2. **By** reciting the prayers which the priest told us.

XII.

Q. What **is** Communion?

A. In Communion we receive **the body, blood,** and soul of our Lord Jesus Christ.

Q. **Must we desire to receive** Communion?

A. Yes, **on** account **of its** great effects in us.

Q. What are the effects of Communion?

A. 1. We are united with Jesus Christ.

2. We become less strong **in evil.**

3. **Hence we are made better.**

4. Telsi koutenliles kyinnemousseltin **lkykel in-**gwilgwiltin.

Q. Letien m etsageel um gest ky mkytsinum?

A. Mous. 1. Gest kakssewissemepsmist.

2. Tel siêuwsum skoukwêts m hoi kakisse illis, hoi m kyksoust.

3. Tessemilko kyspoos kakysposeminum glo Jesus Christ.

4. Nêgŏ tky skeltils kyksglakomin gloskoutŏnt Jesus Christ.

Q. Letien glo tyje skwys glo ntliltien tyje lspoos o inkytsīnum?

A. Essenshiïtsin tyje : gwitsshummis Jesus **Christ** letsgwêlemin.

Q. Stem tglo elg kakskolum **glo tsi** autsi kysin-kytsinum?

A. 1. Kykskamsinum Jesus Christ.

2. Kyksauwauwntshaumin **noningwênctin, inne-**mousselstin, ingamenshêlistin, popoossenstin.

Q. Letien um kytsageel **glo kwemt** kyksgwitsils Jesus Christ skeltits?

A. 1. Kytlêttshumstum ky tigoutst.

2. Ky insippesummêsum.

3. Ky kanmintem.

Q. Letien um kytsageel ne kywisinkytsinum?

A. 1. Kykselêntem glo Jesus Christ.

2. Tessemilko kyspoos, **kakysposiminum** Jesus Christ.

3. Kyksgalitilglum, glo kyssigâpetsinum.

4. Hope of eternal life is increased.

Q. How shall we communicate well?

A. 1. We must have confessed well.

2. From midnight we cannot eat or drink.

3. We must with our whole heart think of Jesus Christ.

4. Even exteriorly we must show how great Jesus Christ is.

Q. What sin does he commit who has a mortal sin in his heart and receives?

A. The greatest sin, he rejects Jesus Christ for the devil.

Q. What more should we do before Communion?

A. 1. We should desire Jesus Christ.

2. We should recite acts of faith, hope, charity, and contrition.

Q. How should we act at the moment when the body of Jesus Christ is given to us?

A. 1. We put out the tongue.

2. We cast down our eyes.

3. We swallow it.

Q. What must we do after Communion?

A. 1. We thank Jesus Christ.

2. We must think of Jesus Christ with all our hearts.

3. We ask for what we need.

15*

4. Um kysauwauwstum ntshaumin noningwênelin, mnemousselstin, ngamenshêlistin.

Q. Letien um etsageel glo shy schalgalt o kysinkytsinum?

A. 1. Kakysiskuttolēminum glo Jesus Christ.

2. Kakystīlien glo kykeltsotin.

FINIS.

4. We recite the prayers of faith, hope, and charity.

Q. How must we act on the day we receive Communion?

A. 1. We must remember Jesus Christ.

2. We must watch over our actions.

THE END.

www.ingramcontent.com/pod-product-compliance
Lightning Source LLC
Chambersburg PA
CBHW030613040726
47497CB00008B/2964